DADDY'S BEST FRIEND

A TEMPERANCE FALLS ROMANCE

LONDON HALE

DADDY'S *best friend*

LONDON HALE

LONDON HALE

*For Edward Cullen and the Twilight fandom,
without which, none of this would have happened.
Sparkle on.*

chapter one

NATHAN

I WASN'T SURE what shit I'd done in my life to be put in this kind of hell, yet there I was. Trying to remain unaffected while Eve—my best friend's daughter and the object of every wet dream I'd had for the past year—walked around in a tiny white dress that barely covered her ass, her legs on full display and her tits pouring out of the neckline.

I'd managed nearly a year without setting foot in this backyard, but Eve's graduation party was something no amount of excuses would permit me to miss. It wasn't like I could say to my best friend, "Hey, man, sorry I can't come. I'm afraid I'll spend the whole time picturing ways to fuck your daughter."

Turned out that fear wasn't unfounded. I was sure if I got close enough to her, I'd be able to see the outline of her nipples through the material of her minuscule dress, because God hated me. Said dress was reminiscent of the nearly nonexistent bikini that had turned everything to shit in the first place. So much so that I'd think she was doing it on purpose if not for the looks she kept shooting the shithead currently panting at her side like a goddamn puppy.

As I watched the two of them together, it took every ounce of self-control I possessed not to storm over and crush his windpipe with my bare hands. The last time I'd see him had been when I'd stopped them for public indecency. I'd never forget the kick to the gut I got when I'd shone the flashlight through the fogged-up window into the back seat of that little shit's car and seen Eve readjusting her clothes, her cheeks flushed pink, her lips bright red and swollen, her nipples hard enough to cut glass.

"Fuck," I muttered under my breath, taking a long pull from my beer, wishing it were whiskey instead. Hell, I'd take any hard liquor at this point—I wasn't picky. Not if I had half a hope of getting through Eve's graduation party with my sanity intact.

"Nate, glad you could make it," Brandon said, clapping a hand on my shoulder.

The rock in my gut solidified as I turned to look at my smiling best friend. He'd been the only person in my life ever to stick around, and how did I repay him? By lusting after his barely legal daughter. Some fucking friend I was.

Swallowing down the bile in my throat, I said, "Hey, man. Nice party."

The backyard was full of more than a hundred

people, fancy shit hanging from the trees and Tiki torches placed throughout his spacious yard. A taco bar and a s'mores station were set up by the outdoor kitchen, and a handful of teenagers tossed beach balls around in the in-ground pool. My only saving grace was that Eve wasn't one of them. There was no fucking way I'd be able to handle seeing her in that bikini again.

Brandon rolled his eyes and smiled in Eve's direction. "Yeah, she didn't want me to make a big deal about it, but I didn't want the day to pass without a celebration. I mean, top ten percent of her class, Nate? My girl's a genius. It's costing me a small fortune, but when it makes her do that"—he gestured to Eve, whose head was thrown back in laughter, her dark hair falling past her ass and her fingers curled around the forearm of Shithead—"I'll give her whatever she wants."

"Never have been able to say no to her," I said.

He just shrugged. Not much he could say to dispute it. Not when I'd been the one by his side for most of the past thirteen years as he'd raised her by himself after her mom split.

"Have you stopped by to say hi to her yet? She was excited you could get the day off work. She's missed you."

Forget a rock—there was a fucking mountain range in my stomach, the jagged tips ripping through my insides. I was an asshole. A disgusting, perverted asshole who didn't deserve these people in my life. Eve had already lost her mother, and because I was a sick fucker who couldn't get a hold of his lust, she had to suffer.

"Nah, she's having fun with her friends. I didn't want to interrupt."

He put his fingers in his mouth and whistled, getting Eve's attention. Once she looked toward her dad, Brandon tilted his head in my direction. The smile that spread across her face hit me with the force of a hurricane. She was genuinely happy to see me, and I'd been spending the past year making any excuse I could to avoid being in her presence.

I watched with smug satisfaction as she left Shithead behind to run toward us, her tits bouncing and barely contained in the low neckline of her dress. *Jesus.* I closed my eyes and took a deep breath, trying my damnedest to get my shit under control.

"Nathan!"

I snapped my eyes open a split second before her body collided with mine, her vanilla and apple scent surrounding me, immediately turning my cock to steel. My arm automatically went around her to catch her while I shifted my hips enough so she couldn't feel exactly what she was doing to me, just by breathing.

"I'm so glad you came," she said, her head resting on my shoulder as she wrapped her arms around me, her feet dangling above the ground.

I held her with one arm, all my concentration focused on two things—not letting her feel my fucking hard-on and not crushing this beer bottle in my fist. After a few seconds, I set her down, stepping back and offering her what was probably more of a grimace than a smile. "Congratulations. Sorry I missed your birthday party last month. I had to work a double."

"Yeah, Dad told me." She fingered the edge of her short as hell dress, and I forced myself not to stare at those silky-smooth legs I wanted nothing more than to feel wrapped around my waist. "You could've stopped by another time. I haven't really seen you in almost a year."

Except that wasn't true, and the blush on her cheeks proved she was thinking exactly what I was. The last time I'd seen her had been in the back seat of a brand-new car that cost more than I made in a year. She darted her eyes to her dad then back to me, the nervousness written clearly on her face.

Before I could reply, the blond shithead strolled up to her, throwing an arm around her shoulder and bringing her into his side. "Hey, babe."

She didn't even glance his way, just kept her eyes on me. My cock twitched in my jeans.

"Nate, have you met Brock?" Brandon asked. "He and Evie have been seeing each other for a few months. He's Clark's kid."

Brock. He even had the name of a shithead. And his parents were assholes. Rich, entitled assholes. Clark Wilkinson might be Brandon's partner, but he was a Grade A douchebag. Despite being bred and groomed in that lifestyle, Brandon had never fit that mold, not in all the years I'd known him. And because of that, neither did Eve. But even with his shortcomings, Brock was better suited for her than I ever would be.

And I hated it.

Narrowing my eyes, I said, "Yeah, I think I've seen him around town once or twice. You drive a brand-new Lexus, don't you?"

Shithead looked at me then, and I had the pleasure of watching the color drain from his face. It was clear he hadn't recognized me before, and now he was sweating bullets, no doubt praying I wouldn't out him to his girlfriend's father about the time he fucked her in the backseat of his car.

I ground my molars together, my jaw ticking with the effort to keep myself in check. Thirteen years ago, I took an oath to serve and protect, and in all that time, my oath had never been tested like it was right now. I wanted to strangle the pretentious little prick with his necktie that probably cost more than my first car, just because of the way he'd been looking at Eve. Like he knew her—knew what her lips tasted like, knew what her smooth skin felt like under his hands, knew the sounds she made when she came. Knew what it was like to be inside all that soft, wet heaven.

Fuck.

"I'm gonna grab another," I said, holding up my empty beer bottle and ducking away.

Just before I went through the back door into the house, I paused and looked over my shoulder at the three of them, if only to remind myself I didn't belong. Not here at this party. Not in this crowd. And certainly not with my best friend's eighteen-year-old daughter.

They were right where I'd left them, Brandon and Shithead talking about something and laughing like old friends, but Eve wasn't joining in.

Instead, she was staring right at me.

chapter two

EVE

AS NATHAN WALKED away, the hug he'd given me   still seared every inch of my body. How I hadn't whimpered when his arm slid around me, I had no idea. I'd wanted to. That hug had lit something inside me I didn't think I could extinguish. Something I didn't even want to try to put out.

"So, my Evie's headed to Yale, my alma mater. Are you following your old man's footsteps, Brock?" my dad asked, apparently talking colleges and majors. Again.

Brock laughed and squeezed me closer before launching into something about Ivy League schools on the East Coast and shared plane rides back, as if he had any right to discuss my future.

But like the good girl I was, I held still so the son of the richest man in town could claim me in a way I could barely stomach. I even smiled to make sure my dad thought everything was fine. Meanwhile, I kept my eyes locked on the retreating police officer across the way. The one who hadn't come to see me in about a year. The one who looked back at me as he reached the door.

I nearly came from that look.

Nathan devoured me with his eyes. There was so much fire in that man. So much restrained passion. I could see it, practically feel it. Everyone else went about their day, blathering on to others as if whatever they talked about was somehow important. Not me. I was pinned, completely caught up in the spell that was Nathan Pearce. Shaky and needy and altogether aroused…by my dad's best friend.

Oh God, that thought only made it worse. Why was that so hot?

Nathan looked away and disappeared inside at the same moment my dad seemed to notice something behind me.

"Brock, your dad's here." The telltale signs of my dad slipping into work mode appeared just like they had at all my birthday parties. And our weekends home together. And every dinner alone with him I could ever remember, when his phone rang or an email came through. "I need to get an answer on that riverfront property deal. You'll hang out with Evie for a few, right?"

Without waiting for a reply, he walked off, which meant Brock had me all to himself. Something he had a tendency to take advantage of. And I wasn't in the mood for it.

"You should probably go say hi," I said, trying to edge away from him. Not that he could take a hint. He moved his arm lower along my back and settled his hand over my hip in a possessive grip. One that felt wrong and out of place. I loved being touched—was actually really affectionate—just not then. And not with Brock.

But when Nathan hugged me…

"I promise not to be gone long," Brock said, whispering into my ear as if I cared where he went. And maybe I would have five minutes ago, before Nathan had wrapped one big, strong arm around me and held me off the ground. Before I'd felt the hard muscles under his clothes. Before I'd noticed something else that was hard about him.

"Take your time," I said. "I need to mingle more."

But Brock had other ideas. "Why don't you go grab me a beer?"

"Uh, because you're not old enough?"

"So what? It's a house party." He reached down and slid his hand up the back of my thigh, teasing under the hem of my skirt. Ignoring my glare and my hand pushing against his chest. "Grab one for yourself, too. We can have a little drink, maybe find a hiding spot in that pool house of yours. I can finally see what's going on under this dress. We just have to avoid the cop your dad hangs with. No one else will care."

His smile should have been charming, but it only made me nauseated. This was Brock—pushy, demanding, spoiled, and not one to take no for an answer very well. Still, beers were in the kitchen. Nathan was in the kitchen. I wanted to be where he was.

"Yeah, okay," I said, to the beer part only. There was no way I was going to be alone with him in the pool house.

Brock had been trying to get into my panties since he moved to Temperance Falls halfway through freshman year. I'd agreed to go out with him a couple of times because he had a wild side to him. I thought I'd like that, but I'd been wrong. And breaking up with the son of your dad's business partner turned out to be a lot harder than I'd thought it would be. We weren't together—not at all—but our dads thought we were, and Brock liked to do whatever he felt was necessary to stay in his daddy's good graces. So he pursued me, and I did everything I could to keep my distance from him. Something that took far more time than it should have, to be honest.

But I didn't want Brock—not as a boyfriend and certainly not as a lover. Brock was just a boy playing the part of an adult, and I wanted more than awkward fumblings and dick pics. I wanted a man who could set my insides on fire with nothing more than a look. One who made me feel safe and cared for. And I knew exactly who that man was.

But before I could make it through the crowd and inside the house where Nathan had gone, I was waylaid by the only person on earth who probably knew exactly why I was following one of our local police officers.

"Where are you heading?" Genesis asked, walking beside me with a huge grin on her face.

"Brock wants a beer."

"Funny. I thought I saw a certain police officer heading this same way just a minute ago."

My face grew warm, and I cursed my pale skin for that telling sign. "Quite the coincidence."

"It is, isn't it?" She bit her lip to try to rein in her smile and nodded toward the crowd of people behind us. "I'll run interference. You've probably got ten minutes before Brock goes chasing after that skirt."

I tugged at said skirt. The one that was way too short. The one I'd put on hoping to attract the attention of someone other than Brock. And if the look Nathan had given me before he'd walked into the house was any indication, the dress had worked. "It's Nathan. Nothing's going to happen."

"You're right. It's Nathan. The man you've secretly crushed on for years." She leaned closer, lowering her voice. "You look hot. He won't be able to ignore the fact that you're an adult now. A woman. Legal."

God, I hoped she was right.

As she walked off in Brock's direction with a huge, fake smile on her face, I took a deep breath and prepared myself for what I was about to do. I'd had a crush on Nathan Pearce for years. I'd assumed it was completely one-sided, and it probably had been. But one night, just six short months ago, Nathan had found Brock and me parked out along the lakefront. In the back seat. Nathan had gone from being my dad's best friend to Officer Pearce in a single moment.

He'd tried to appear professional and intimidating when he'd yanked the two of us out and read us the riot act about how dangerous and stupid we were being, but I'd seen through him. He'd been angry. Almost possessive of me. That had piqued my interest and made me wonder if…just if.

Nathan was more than twice my age, though, and he was my dad's best friend. Two relationship killers, for sure. Plus, there was no way he'd want someone like me—I was too young, too naïve. Too innocent. I hadn't even given up my V-card yet. Nathan would want a woman, not a little girl. Even if that girl was eighteen. At least, that had been what I'd told myself.

But then he'd hugged me today, and he'd been hard and trying not to let me feel it. He wanted something. I just had to figure out a way to get him to tell me what, exactly, because I'd give it to him. I'd give him anything.

Eventually, I slipped into the kitchen and quietly closed the door behind me. Nathan was leaning against the counter on the other side of the room. His head hung down, his short-cropped hair looking even darker than normal. The ridiculous island with the white marble top blocked my view of his legs, but his chest and shoulders were fully on display under the dark collared shirt he'd worn. He was normally a T-shirt and jeans guy, so the sight of that collar told me he'd tried to look nice. Perhaps to dress up a little.

I preferred the T-shirts.

As he took a deep breath and sighed, I spotted the beer he'd come inside to retrieve in his hand. But it was unopened.

"Did you have trouble finding the opener?"

His head flew up, and his eyes met mine. Deep and dark and so very tortured.

"I…no, I'm good. Thanks, Eve."

I crept forward, keeping my eyes on his. "You know you're the only person who calls me Eve? Everyone else says Evie."

"I figured turnabout was fair play. You're the only person who calls me Nathan." He twisted off the top and took a swig of his beer, finally looking away when he pulled the bottle from his lips. "What are you doing in here, anyway? Shouldn't you be outside enjoying your party?"

I shrugged. "I don't know all those people. Besides, they're not here for me."

His lips turned up in a small, lopsided smile. "They're here for your dad." He always had been able to see through the bullshit people tried to hide behind. Maybe that was the cop in him, or maybe it was just Nathan.

"Exactly." I slid into the space between him and the island. Too close for social norms, too far away for my preference. "Why are *you* hiding in here?"

"Needed air."

"You were outside."

He glanced behind me, probably through the window over the sink. The one that looked out over the backyard. "Those people are stifling."

"Yeah, they are." I leaned forward, getting right up in his space. "Hey, Nathan?"

He didn't move away. "Yeah?"

"Why haven't you been coming around?"

A shrug. "Been busy."

"Lie."

"Eve," he said, almost sighing my name.

The sound sent shivers down my spine, so I mimicked him. After I wrapped my hands around his wrist to tug him closer. "Nathan."

He closed his eyes for a second, looking conflicted, though he certainly didn't pull out of my grip. "What are you doing?"

What was I doing? I'd come in to check. To see if what I thought I'd seen and felt outside had been a figment of my imagination. But it hadn't, as evidenced by the bulge he was obviously sporting, and I needed to figure out what to do with that information.

So I answered honestly. "Pushing you."

"Pushing me to do what, exactly?"

"Whatever it is you want."

"Why?"

"Because you look like a man who needs to be pushed."

His eyes devoured me again, burning me from the inside out. Leaving nothing but ash where I'd once stood. "Maybe I'm the one man you shouldn't push."

Too late. "Nathan?"

"Yeah?"

"Why are you looking at my lips?"

His jaw clenched, his eyes darting back to mine. "I'm not."

But he was, and we both knew it. Which meant… "Do you want to kiss me?"

A muscle in his jaw ticked. I'd seen that tic a thousand times, knew it as a sign of his frustration. Of his control being worked hard. That was a tic of need.

"You do," I said, smiling as I inched closer and dragged my hand farther up his arm. "You want to kiss me."

His hands landed on my hips, gripping hard. "I want…to do a lot of things with you. But we can't." His words didn't match his hands, which were pulling me in with every breath.

"Why not?"

Another jaw tic. "Your age."

"I'm eighteen."

"Barely."

"Eighteen and one day or eighteen and three hundred and fifty days is still eighteen."

He sighed. "I'm not eighteen, Eve."

"I know." I gripped him by his belt loops, tugging. Refusing to let him go.

But still, he resisted. "Your dad's my best friend."

"He'd never have to worry that you wouldn't treat me right." I ran the back of my fingers over the bulge in his pants, the one he'd been trying to keep me from noticing. The one he'd been sporting since he hugged me. He grabbed my wrist, but he didn't try to stop me. Didn't pull away from my touch. So I did it again, harder. Longer.

"Would you, Nathan?" I pressed as I slipped

my finger under the collared shirt he wore. Tickling through the hair leading down to what I really wanted to get a feel of. "Would you take care of me?"

He moved his hands to cup my arms. Whether to hold me closer or push me away, I wasn't sure. "You know I would. I'd do anything for you. But not this."

I leaned forward, pushing on my tiptoes and pressing my lips to his in the softest, sweetest kiss I could give him. "Not what? Kiss me? I know you want to. I know you want to do a lot more than kiss, too."

He groaned and closed his eyes, the grip on my arms tightening. Giving me just the right amount of pain. I hoped he left marks. I wanted his claim on my body any way I could get it.

When he opened his eyes again, they were molten. "Anyone can see if they look through the window."

"They'll think we're talking. They won't know what I do with my hands."

Which was true, and that gave me an idea of what I could do with more than my hands. I hadn't ever given a guy a blow job, but I wanted to. Needed. Craved the taste of this man on my tongue like nothing else. If I couldn't kiss his lips…

I dropped to my knees.

"Eve." He said my name like a warning, but I just grinned up at him as I unfastened his jeans, pushing them down his thighs to free his erection. He wasn't wearing underwear, which made my job all that much easier. It was as if he'd planned or hoped for this—or something like it—to happen. That thought had such an effect on me my panties grew wet. Not damp, not warm, not that disgusting M-word no one liked. They were totally and completely wet.

I couldn't wait for him to feel how much, but first, it was his turn.

Nathan held still, watching and wary as I teased him with my fingers. I'd done this much once with Brock—slid my hand inside his pants to feel a dick for the first time. I'd had no frame of reference then, nothing from real life to compare him to. Sure, I'd seen pictures and video clips online, but I'd never gotten up close and personal with a man. Brock had been my first touch, and I was so glad he was because I knew what to do. Sort of.

That boy had nothing on Nathan.

He was so hard, so long. Soft to the touch but solid underneath. But it wasn't the length that made my eyes widen and my heart beat faster. It was the width. Thick was an understatement. Nothing in my modest toy drawer compared to him; nothing I'd ever even thought about taking inside me came close.

When I couldn't wait anymore, when I was desperate to feel with more than just my fingertips, I slid my hand around the base of that impressive dick and stroked upward. All the way to the tip. Precome gathered at the slit, enticing me. Making me want to kiss, to lick, to taste.

"Eve." The breathless, growly way he said my name set me on fire.

I leaned in, ready, shaking with my need to

devour him. He was so close to the edge, so tense as he tried to hold himself back, but I was going to break him. I had to.

"Let me," I pleaded just before I pressed a kiss right to the tip of his hard, heavy erection. "Let me."

chapter three

NATHAN

HOW IN THE fuck had we gotten here? All I'd needed was an escape so I could get my dick in check. Just some goddamn peace and quiet so I could get my head in the fucking game again—remind myself why I couldn't snatch Eve away from Shithead and claim her right there in front of everyone.

But I'd wanted to.

Christ, more than anything, I'd wanted to wipe that smug grin off his pretty-boy face. With my fist. Break every one of his fucking fingers when he'd wrapped his arm around her and tugged her into his side.

And now here she was, on her knees in front of me, and I couldn't do anything but stare. I should've stopped her. If I were a better man—a *stronger* man—I would've. Instead, I watched with rapt attention as those full lips kissed the tip of my cock, her bubble-gum tongue flicking out to lick at the head.

"Let me," she begged.

And I was gone.

I was so fucking gone for this girl.

I fumbled to set my beer bottle on the counter, then reached out and brushed her hair back from her face, gathering the long, dark strands in my hand as she continued to tease me. She licked me like a lollipop, her tongue eager and clumsy, her unpolished enthusiasm only illustrating exactly how young she was.

That thought alone shouldn't have tightened my balls the way it did.

Mad at her for putting me in this position—mad at *myself* for not having the willpower to stop it—I tightened my hand in her hair. "If you're going to do it, do it. Open up and let me slide my cock between those pretty pink lips."

She groaned, her eyes flashing up to mine, a flush covering her cheeks. Reaching out, she rested her hands on my thighs, balancing herself. And then she did as I told her, engulfing the tip of my cock in her mouth.

"*Jesus.*"

The sight alone was enough to make my knees weak—her lips stretched taut around me and her sky-blue eyes staring up into mine—but combine it with the heaven that was her mouth, and I didn't stand a fucking chance. I'd had all of seven seconds between her lips, and I already needed to go off down her throat. I was a grown man—a grown man who hadn't gotten a blow job in months, but a grown man nonetheless. And yet I felt like I was no better than those little douchebags she went to school with who didn't know the meaning of delayed gratification.

I knew plenty about delayed gratification.

Watching her prance around in her tiny dresses, her perky tits taunting me even in my dreams, but not letting myself do anything about it. I'd had a full year of wanting but not taking, and the deprivation was bubbling under my skin, threatening to boil over at any second.

I was so tired of wanting. I needed to *have*.

I reached down and stroked her face with one hand while I used my other to guide her head with a fistful of her hair. When I tightened my grip, she let out a groan, the sound reverberating down my length, sending shock waves through me. I clenched my jaw and held on to the frayed string that was my control as her tongue lapped at the underside of my cock.

She dug her fingernails into my skin through the denim, and I couldn't deny how much I loved knowing this turned her on. Her tits, barely constrained in her dress, were heaving and flushed. She kept shifting her hips, her fingers restless against my thighs, like all she wanted to do was reach down and finger herself. Get herself off to sucking my cock.

It made me want to tug her up just so I could slip my hand under her dress and feel how wet she was. How swollen. How hot to fuck.

She lapped at me, sucked me into her mouth, trying to go deeper with each pass. Her approach wasn't smooth or practiced, her eyes tearing when she tried to take more than half my cock, but she was eager as hell. Knowing she wanted this as badly as I did made me want to spill all over her tongue.

"Easy, baby, easy," I said, pulling back so she could catch her breath.

She didn't even let me get out of her mouth before she was diving back in, her cheeks hollowing as she sucked me hard.

How many times had she done this? How many guys had experienced this—knew what kind of nirvana rested behind those perfect lips? The thought brought out an animalistic hunger in me I'd never known before. I wanted to have her. Mark her. *Claim* her.

I wanted exactly what I couldn't have—what I *shouldn't* have.

Not able to look at those crystal-clear blue eyes staring up at me for another second, I lifted my gaze to stare out the window. Shithead was standing in the middle of the yard, looking around. Probably for the girl currently on her knees in front of me, anxious to take my come down her throat. The thought of her going up to him later, still tasting me on her tongue, had me thrusting into her mouth faster.

I glanced down at Eve again. Her eyes were still trained on me, her cheeks hollowed out, and only one hand rested against my leg. The other was moving under her pretty white dress.

The orgasm slammed into me like a wrecking ball, even when I lifted my eyes from the temptation at my feet.

"Fuck, Eve. *Fuck.*"

As I stared outside, my cock still emptying in her mouth, I spotted Brandon standing near Eve's friend Gen and Shithead. Brandon said something to them, then turned toward the house. Even though I was sure he couldn't see into the kitchen with the blinding sun from outside, it still felt like he was looking right at me.

While I was coming down the throat of his little girl.

What kind of bastard was I? I'd taken advantage of her, hadn't even tried to stop her when she'd gone down and tugged my cock out. Christ, I hadn't even given her the choice to take my come in her mouth or not.

I'd taken her like an animal.

The heaven I'd felt for the past ten minutes burned up, leaving me once again in purgatory.

"Shit. *Shit.*" I pulled back, my still half-hard cock slipping from between her lips, and shoved myself in my jeans before turning my back on her. "Goddammit. I'm sorry. I shouldn't have done that."

She gasped behind me, but I couldn't bring myself to comfort her. Couldn't turn around to offer her any kind of reassurance. Couldn't even stand to look into her eyes. I'd just fucked the mouth of my best friend's daughter. I'd come down her throat.

And I'd loved every fucking minute of it.

I was a sick bastard, and I needed to get away from her as fast as I could, before I dragged her down with me.

"I'm sorry," I said again, because I couldn't give her anything else.

I didn't look back as I strode through the house and left out the front door, not knowing how I was going to make this right. But I knew with certainty the first step was staying as far as fucking possible away from my own personal Garden of Eden.

chapter four

EVE

THERE WAS SOMETHING utterly humiliating about being left on the floor with the taste of a man's come on your tongue and your own hand as wet as your panties. I hadn't been fast enough to chase after Nathan, hadn't even made it to my feet before he was already out the door. So I'd sat, and I'd wallowed in all my debauched glory.

"I hate to interrupt you two, but… Whoa." Gen froze, her eyes widening before she jumped into action. Without another word, she peeked back over her shoulder before quickly closing the door behind her. "What the hell happened in here?"

Ugh, I must have looked like quite the sight for that sort of reaction. Thank God Brock or my dad hadn't walked in with her. I pressed my back against the cabinet, pulled my knees up to my chest, and rested my cheek against them so I didn't have to see her face when I told her.

"He left."

The clock in the foyer ticked in the resulting silence, the sound booming in my head as I waited for Gen to respond. To help me figure out what had gone so wrong. Because I couldn't—I had no idea why he'd left me the way he had.

"What do you mean he left?"

My eyes burned, humiliation making me want to cry. "I don't know. One second, he was coming in my mouth. The next, he was gone."

Gen's face appeared before mine, her head cocked to look me in the eye. "You gave him a beej?"

I sniffed. "Yeah."

"And he just left? Did he at least say thank you?"

"No. He said he was sorry, and then he walked out the door." I sighed and brought my head up, knocking it into the cabinet behind me with a quiet thud. "I thought he wanted me."

"Honey, there's no way that man didn't want you. I saw the way he was looking at you earlier."

"Then why'd he leave? Was I so horrible at it that he—" I bit my lip to cut off the words. Had I done something wrong? Had my inexperienced fumblings somehow disgusted him or made him change his mind? He'd been into it, been aroused by me. So then why did he say he shouldn't have let me? Why did he run off and leave me crumpled on the floor like nothing? Like garbage.

"Evie," Gen said. "You're seriously not going to

let him run away, are you? He's just scared. I mean, shit, he let you blow him in *your dad's* house. That's gotta mess with his mind, even if he is a badass, totally hot, and fuckable cop. With all those muscles and that tattoo."

I could have rolled my eyes. "Would you stop with the tattoo?"

"It's a woman holding a fucking apple. With *Eve* holding an apple. Hello."

"It's a scene from the bible, *Genesis*," I replied, stressing her full first name. "That doesn't mean it's because of me."

"Whatever." She scoffed, then braced herself on the island, fanning her face. "*Jesus*. I can't believe you had his cock in your mouth." She pointed a finger in my direction. "I hope you know I want details as soon as you're emotionally stable enough to give them. Especially once you push him past his fears and get really naughty with him."

Fears. That word reverberated in my mind. Forcing pieces of the puzzle that was Nathan and me to realign and show me a different picture. Nathan was afraid of us together? Could that be all? Her words made sense, at least. Nathan and my dad had been friends forever, had never really fought, and had always been there for one another. They were practically brothers. But I'd never called him uncle, never seen him like that. He was Nathan, and he cared about me. Before I got on my knees and after. If he was having a hard time accepting what we'd done, I needed to talk to him. To help him see how good we were together. I needed to make him look me in the eye and not run. Immediately, before his head got in the way.

But my graduation party was in full swing, and my car was thoroughly blocked by all the guests' vehicles. Good thing my best friend trusted me.

"Do you have your keys?" I asked as I got to my feet. My dress was a wrinkled mess, but it didn't matter. No one but Gen and Nathan were going to see me this way. Not if I managed to get to him in time.

"Yeah, why?"

"I need to go to Nathan's."

"Right *now*? You're kind of in the middle of a graduation party, in case you didn't notice all the arrogant assholes in your backyard."

I glanced up to look out the window, standing exactly where Nathan had been when I'd been on my knees. He'd had a clear shot into the backyard full of the snooty people. Hell, I could even see my dad out there.

I could see my dad.

"What's wrong?" Gen asked, coming to stand beside me and stare out the same window.

"He was here. He was standing right here when I…"

She raised her eyebrows and looked back at me. "You think that's what made him run?"

I had no idea, but it wasn't an illogical jump to assume he'd seen something out there that reminded him of where we were. Of who we were to each other. Or who we'd been, because I'd never go back to just being little Eve, daughter of his best friend. I wanted more than that, and deep down, I knew he did, too.

"Cover for me? I need to go see him." I held out my hand, knowing Gen would come through. She always did. It took her a second of watching me with wary eyes, but she finally sighed and dug into her pocket.

"Yeah, all right. I'll go with the 'lady problems' excuse. Gets 'em every time." She handed me her keys before pulling me into her arms for a hug. One I desperately needed. "Be careful. And remember, I will fuck him up if he hurts my bestie."

"Thanks." I hurried for the front door, hoping none of the guests would catch me before I could slip out. "And hey, I owe you one."

"Maybe Nate has some hot friends and we can double." Her laughter followed me through the front door, cutting off as it closed behind me.

The front yard was thankfully clear of guests, and I was in Gen's car and turning onto the road before anyone spotted me. You could circle the entire island that made up Temperance Falls in about twenty minutes, so the drive to Nathan's took almost no time at all even though he lived on the opposite side. I turned just before the factory entrance and followed the blacktopped road to the end, a trek I'd made as a passenger a thousand times.

Nathan lived on a cul-de-sac—one of only three houses on his stretch of road. All small, squat little ranches with grass front yards and chain link fences between them. His sat on the far left and backed up to a patch of woods that blocked him from the water's edge.

I'd always loved his house. Even as a little girl, it had seemed so much warmer and more inviting than the one I actually grew up in. And when we'd moved from that huge house to the monstrosity my dad currently called home, I'd craved this little white house tucked into the trees even more.

This house had always been more of a home to me than my own.

Nathan's car was pulled all the way around back, parked against the garage at the rear of the property. That sight caused the butterflies in my stomach to take flight. He was definitely home. There would be no avoiding, no running, no hiding from the conversation we needed to have. I was about to push my way into Nathan's house and make him talk to me.

Once I caught my breath.

With one last sigh and a mental pep talk even Gen would have been proud of, I turned off the ignition and stepped out of her car. This was it. I couldn't back down. I couldn't show weakness. If I wanted Nathan, I'd need to make that clear. To prove to him that we could work.

I needed to be brave.

chapter five

NATHAN

I COULDN'T GET away from Brandon's house fast enough. What I really wanted to do was bail, escape somewhere else, but this island was like a goddamn prison. If I didn't want everyone in my business, I either needed to hop a ferry or a puddle jumper to the city, or I needed to lock myself in my house.

That was fine. I had a full bottle of Jack waiting to keep me company at home.

Going from Brandon's neighborhood to mine was always a shock—sprawling estates with professionally landscaped yards to worn houses with peeling paint and weeds cut down to resemble grass. I'd never spent much time thinking about the differences, other than the obvious. It'd always been like that—since we became friends as freshmen in high school. He was the son of a goddamned senator, and I was an orphan.

In school, he'd been quarterback of the football team, president of the student body, and the motherfucking homecoming king. I'd been the kid setting the chemistry lab on fire and getting high between classes.

The differences only became more pronounced as we'd grown up. When he'd gone to college, I'd gone into the army. When he'd been working his first job post-graduation, probably making more than I made now, I'd been at the police academy. While he was wining and dining clients, I was chasing down criminals and locking them up. We were like night and day, but somehow, despite that, we'd been best friends for more than twenty years.

And I'd just mouth-fucked his baby girl in his house.

"*Fuck*." I slammed my hand on my steering wheel as I pulled into my driveway before throwing the car into Park. Once inside my house, I went straight to the cabinet above the refrigerator and pulled down the unopened bottle of whiskey. I wasn't going to think about the fact that Brandon had gotten it for me for my birthday, and I was now using it to forget the feel of his daughter's lips around my cock, her tongue stroking my shaft.

Tossing the cap on the counter, I took a long swig from the bottle, scrubbing a hand over my head. I couldn't believe I'd given in. Twelve months of deprivation down the drain because a pretty girl in a pretty dress put her hands on me and I didn't have the self-control to say no.

But it hadn't been just a pretty girl. It'd been Eve.

Even her name was a temptation. Of course, I had to fall for the one and only woman on the island who was off-limits to me.

It didn't matter how much I fought it, though. She was always there, in the back of my mind. I didn't want to admit it, but she'd been getting under my skin for a couple of years, with her free-flowing smiles and her laughter that always seemed to be directed at me. She'd never talked to me like I was her dad's best friend. I was just Nathan to her. There had never been anything sexual between us—at least not on my end. I'd never thought of her that way. Not until that pool party last summer. Not until every asset of hers I'd had blinders to was on full display courtesy of a see-through white bikini.

The age difference didn't matter to my cock. The fact that she was part of the only family I had didn't matter, either.

She was the ray of sunshine in a lifetime of darkness. How could I not be drawn to her?

I headed into the living room, drinking from the bottle as I went. Even after several mouthfuls of whiskey, my limbs loosening enough so my muscles weren't pulled taut, I could still smell her. So strongly, it was like she'd walked right past me. My cock was rock hard at her scent, like Pavlov's fucking dog. I grabbed the hem of my shirt and lifted it to my nose, breathing in apples and vanilla. *Eve.*

Setting the bottle on my coffee table, I yanked the shirt off over my head and threw it aside. I closed my eyes and thought of Eve on her knees in front of me, a flush covering her face, her lips parted and bright red. I'd tossed her aside as easily as that shirt. I'd left her on her *knees*. I'd walked away without anything more than a bullshit apology. Some fucking man I was.

A knock sounded at the door, pulling me from my thoughts. I strode to the front window and looked out, seeing Gen's car parked along the curb. There was no way it was Gen on my porch, though. I should've expected Eve to hunt me down. Once that girl got her mind set on something, she sank her teeth in. My cock only hardened further at that fact, knowing how much she wanted this. Wanted me.

Scrubbing a hand over my face, I sighed and opened the door. There she stood, all clenched fists and bravado. Her lips were still puffy from being stretched around my dick, her hair a little disheveled from when I'd had the strands clutched in my fist. How the fuck was I supposed to hold a civil conversation with that memory fresh in my mind?

"What are you doing here, Eve?" I said a little harsher than I should've.

Her entire demeanor changed, her shoulders deflating along with her face, and I wanted to snatch the words back. Could I do *anything* right by this girl?

"I...I thought..." She took a deep breath, balling up those fists again, rolling her shoulders as she stood to her full height and tilted her head up to stare me right in the eye. So fiery, my Eve. "We need to talk about what happened."

She didn't wait for me to respond, just pushed past me into my house. I closed my eyes and shut the door behind her, gripping the doorknob until my knuckles turned white. I was walking a tightrope over the mouth of a volcano. One wrong step—one wrong *breath*—and I was done.

Turning around to face her, I said, "I'm sorry. I shouldn't have left you like that."

"You're right. You shouldn't have. That's not what I want—"

"But that doesn't change the fact that we shouldn't have done it. I shouldn't have allowed it. I shouldn't have taken advantage of you like that."

"Is that what this is about?" She stormed up to me, looking so tiny this close. Her head didn't even reach my shoulders, but the way she was narrowing her eyes, shoving her finger into my chest, it was as if she were seven feet tall. "You didn't take advantage of me, Nathan. I'm the one who got on her knees, remember?"

"Oh Christ," I groaned, clenching my eyes shut. Except that didn't help because all I saw behind my closed lids were those bright blue eyes of hers looking up at me, her lips wrapped around my cock. I could still feel the velvet heat of her tongue stroking along my length. *Fuck.* Blinking open my eyes, I rubbed a hand over my mouth. "I remember. And I loved it, but I'm twice as old as you are and—"

"You loved it?" she asked, her tone one of amazement. Then her lips quirked up on one side as she trailed her finger down my bare chest, firing sparks along the way. "Really?"

I grabbed her hand, stilling her before she could

get to the waistband of my jeans. "Of course, I loved it. Have you ever given a blow job and *not* had the guy love it?" I asked, then immediately regretted it. The thought of her doing that with any other guy—with *Brock*—made me want to beat every single boy who'd known her like that to a bloody pulp. "Never mind. Don't answer that."

She narrowed her eyes and dropped the smile from her mouth, snatching her hand away. "So you only loved it because you got off. Not because of any sort of connection to me."

I blew out a deep breath, having no idea how to answer this question honestly while still holding on to the tiny shred of sanity I had. "No, that's not what I meant, Eve." How did I tell her I hadn't come that fast since I was fifteen? That, despite her awkward attempts, it was the hottest blow job I'd ever gotten? It wasn't because it was a warm, wet mouth to fuck. It was because it was *her*. "We *shouldn't* have a connection. Not this kind. Not the kind that makes me want to bend you over the couch and fuck you until you're hoarse from screaming my name. Do you know how depraved that is? You're barely legal, on top of being my best friend's *daughter*. And I've been trying to fight it. I really have, but I need you to try with me. I can't do it on my own."

"No. I'm not fighting it. I *want* you to bend me over that couch." She bit the corner of her lip, her cheeks flushing pink as she slid her eyes over to the piece of furniture and back to me. "I mean…maybe not my first time. But I want it. I want it all with you."

"You're only eighteen! You can't know—" I cut off abruptly as her words caught up with me. My heart pounded in my ears, my cock thrumming right along with it. "Wait. What do you mean, your first time?"

She ducked her head, her fingers playing with the hem of her wrinkled dress. The blush of her cheeks spread down her neck and to her chest, disappearing under the neckline. Did her tits flush that pretty pink, too?

"What do you think I mean? I haven't done"— she waved a hand toward my couch—"that."

Sweet fucking Christ, this was not happening to me. I'd been wrong—her backyard wasn't hell. I was in it right now. Eve, in her pretty white dress, smelling like apples, telling me her cherry was mine for the taking? Pure. Fucking. Hell.

I reached out and grabbed her hand, tugging her toward me. She stumbled forward, nearly crashing into my chest, her fingers resting just above the waistband of my jeans. "Are you telling me you've never been fucked, Eve?"

Her lips parted, her breaths coming quick. She brushed unknown patterns on my skin, and I wanted her hand lower, lower, *lower*. Wished I'd never stopped her in the first place.

"No, I've never been *fucked*, Nathan."

"But that night… When I caught you and that shithead in the back seat…" I clenched my teeth at the memory, seeing Eve disheveled and obviously aroused.

"I didn't…we didn't, um, you know." She lifted

one shoulder in a shrug. "We just messed around a little."

The thought of that fucker having his hands on her at all was enough to make me want to strangle him, but I got a smug satisfaction knowing she hadn't allowed him that part of herself. In all her eighteen years, this perfect, beautiful, intelligent girl had never felt another man inside her. And she wanted the first time she experienced it to be with me.

I tried to swallow the gravel in my throat, but it didn't help. My words came out strangled and rough. "Why now? Why me?"

She stepped closer, pressing our bodies together and placing a kiss at the center of my chest. "It's always been you. You're the only man I've ever felt safe with. I'm home with you. Why can't you see that?"

It was on the tip of my tongue to ask her why she couldn't pick someone like Shithead. Why she couldn't pick someone worthy of her—someone who could give her the life she was accustomed to—but I didn't have it in me. I didn't deserve this—didn't deserve *her*—but I was tired of fighting it, despite the consequences. I was tired of pushing her away when it was clear she wanted this connection as much as I did.

"If we do this, we can't ever take it back. Things are going to change forever. Once I have you, Eve…" I shook my head, clenching my hands into fists to stop from reaching toward her. From grasping those lush hips I wanted to dig my fingers into. She had to realize what this meant. What she was saying if she said yes. "Once I have you, I'm not going to let anyone else even *look* at you. You'll be mine."

Her lips parted as she looked up at me. "I want to be yours. I've *always* wanted to be yours."

I groaned and couldn't stop myself from reaching for her, bending down and gripping her under her ass to lift her to my mouth. I crashed my lips against hers, swallowing her gasp as I slipped my tongue inside and tasted her for the first time—an intoxicating mix of marshmallows and me, and that only fueled my need even more.

I'd fantasized about this hundreds of times, but even those fantasies didn't stand up to the reality of Eve. Experienced or not, she poured everything she had into the kiss, throwing her arms around my shoulders and clinging to me as she moaned into my mouth with every stroke of her tongue against mine. She wrapped her legs around my waist, grinding her pussy against my cock that always seemed to be hard around her. And right now, as I felt how warm and wet she was even through the layers of fabric we wore, I wondered how in the hell I'd ever had the power to stay away from her for so long. Before, I never knew what I'd been missing. But now that I'd had a taste? I didn't think I'd ever be able to let her go.

After making it to my bedroom and kicking the door shut behind me, I strode to my bed. She yelped when I tossed her on it, then caged her in, my hands resting on either side of her head.

Leaning over her, I nipped a path down her neck, then inhaled deeply at the curve of her shoulder.

"You smell like *apples*, Eve. Do you do that shit on purpose?"

She breathed out a laugh, digging her nails into my back as she tried to pull me closer. "It's my body wash. Gen buys it for me because of the whole Eve and the apple thing."

"Of course she does. Just one more thing reminding me what a temptation you are. I smell you everywhere I go—I could still smell you on my shirt when I got home. I can't ever get away from you. I get hard every time I eat an apple, for fuck's sake."

"Is that why you—" She stopped midsentence, darting her eyes to my left arm, then back at me again.

"Is that why I what?" I asked, trailing my fingers along the deep V of her dress.

"It's just…Gen has this theory that this tattoo is somehow for me."

She traced the lines of my half sleeve, running her fingers over the rays of sunlight, then along the profile of the girl's face at the forefront, her delicate hand holding an apple. Yeah, that was my Eve. Not really sure how I'd managed to have this for a year and not have anyone draw the same conclusion.

"Gen's a smart girl," I said, then replaced my fingers along her neckline with my tongue. She trembled beneath me, digging her fingers into my arm.

"Oh God," she said, practically moaning her words. "That is so…sweet."

"*Sweet?*" I scoffed, shaking my head. This tattoo was the furthest thing from sweet. Me getting it? Even worse. "It's depraved, Eve. Even while I was sitting in the chair getting you permanently inked on me, I knew I shouldn't be. But I didn't care. You make me lose my fucking mind."

"Then we're even, because I've been lost over you for too long." She arched into me, pulling me closer.

Hearing her say the words had me frozen in place. Eve was a smart, methodical girl. I knew this wasn't just a passing thing for her. Still, I wanted to know what *too long* meant to her. "How long?"

"Remember the white bikini?"

I groaned, resting my forehead against the curve of her neck. "How can I forget it? You visit me wearing it every time I sleep." Then a thought hit me and I pulled back, narrowing my eyes at her. "Did you *plan* that?"

She bit her lip, looking like the sweetest temptation. "I wanted to see if you'd notice me as more than some little girl."

I didn't know whether to be pissed at her or thankful. She'd put me in an uncomfortable situation—one I never could've given in to...one I never would've given in to. Not when she was underage. But if she hadn't done it, I didn't know if we'd be here now, with her under me and about five seconds from being naked.

"That's fucked up, Eve. You know that, right?"

"Maybe." She shrugged, not looking the least bit remorseful. "But it got us here, didn't it?"

"I can't be mad at anything you do if it ends with you naked in my bed."

"Looks like you've still got some work to do on

the naked part," she said, hooking her leg over my ass and trying to tug me down to settle between her spread thighs.

I brushed my lips over the hard point of her nipple through the material of her dress. "You trying to get me to press my cock against you right now?"

She whimpered, her teeth digging into her lip as she stared up at me, that leg never ceasing its pull. I wanted to do so many things to her, wanted to strip her down and see what she had hiding under this scrap of material.

"If you want me to fuck you, you need to use the words. I don't want you to be embarrassed with me. You don't ever have to be."

She studied me for long moments, her eyes darting between mine, her hands restless against my chest. Her breaths came in short bursts, but still, she just stared, like she was working up the courage to say the words.

Then finally, *finally,* she said, "I'm not embarrassed. I want this. I want you." She paused, licked her lips, and locked her eyes with mine. "I want you to fuck me, Nathan."

chapter six

EVE

THERE WAS SOMETHING so freeing about admitting to Nathan exactly what I wanted. And though I'd never thought I'd use a word like fuck to describe such an act, saying it felt good. It felt right. Because it was what he wanted to hear.

"Shit," Nathan hissed, all breathy and rough. He rolled his hips into mine, grinding hard against all the right spots, making me groan and grab for him. "I'm gonna fuck you so good. *So* good. By the time we're done, my name's going to be the only word you remember."

Oh God. No one had ever talked to me like that, but I loved it. Loved the way his filthy words made me feel, made me want. I kissed him once, tangling my tongue with his before he tore himself away.

"Need a taste, baby." Nathan's mouth burned a

trail down my neck, his touch soft as he brushed his lips against my skin. As he tasted me. The neckline of my dress didn't stop him from sinking farther. He kept kissing, blowing hot air through the fabric and warming my skin in a way that made me shiver. Teasing me in the worst way. I wanted his mouth on me, wanted to feel him without the fabric between us. But he just kept going, kept sucking, kept breathing. All the way until he reached the fullest part of my breast. With his hand on the underside, he brought his mouth down on my nipple. Sucking. Pulling fabric and flesh into his mouth, using his teeth until I gasped and arched into him.

"Nathan." I choked as he gave me one more tease before he pulled away.

"These tits have haunted me since your birthday party last year. Every time I closed my eyes, all I could see was the outline of your nipples through those tiny white triangles." He fell silent long enough for me to look down, to seek him out. His eyes burned into mine as he brought his hand up, running a finger along the neckline of my dress. "I kept wondering if they tasted as good as they looked."

I couldn't look away, didn't even want to blink as he tugged down the neckline of my dress. The tension pulled my straps, tightening the fabric along my back and shoulders almost to the point of pain. I didn't wince, though. Didn't try to stop him. I wanted this as much as he did.

Almost in slow motion, Nathan leaned down, following the white fabric as it descended along my skin. The scruff on his chin scratched along the top of my breast like a warning. A dark sky over flat waters, the possibility of a storm kicking up almost a certainty. I wasn't going to head for cover, though. I'd wanted to be in the middle of it, wanted to feel the wind and the wet of Nathan's tempest, to dance with the thunder and let the lightning crash along my skin. I'd wanted it, and I was about to have it.

Nathan's storm started as many did. Not with a bang or a crash, not with a violent crest that incited the fury. No, his started with a single raindrop—a light, wet kiss right on the tip of my nipple. Once. Twice. Three times. He added his tongue, his eyes staying on mine as he licked me. I held tight to the pillow, watching him. Hungry for him.

He opened his mouth, and I locked down my body. Every muscle clenched as he inched lower, as he brought his lips to my breast. As he pulled my nipple into his mouth and sent sparks of sensation flying through my body with one long, hard suck.

"Shit." I bit my lip to keep from screaming his name.

"Your skin tastes like fucking apples, Eve. So sweet." Nathan groaned against me, rolling to his side as he inched lower. His hands were warm and gentle as they ran up my thighs, taking the skirt of my dress with them. I grabbed the pillow under my head and held on, watching him. Waiting for whatever he was planning to do to me. Every inch of my skin on fire, my pussy wet, and my heart racing. This would be no awkward, fumbling, teenage grope session. I could tell just by the look in Nathan's eyes as he tugged at the sides of my panties.

"Cute," he said, dragging a finger just under the lace trim of my white cotton panties, never quite touching where I needed it. "Perfect."

I waited for him to take them off, to tug them right down my legs so he could see all of me. But Nathan had other plans. He teased me through the fabric, letting the storm brew a little longer, letting it build.

With every pass, he practically killed me. Never directing his touch to where I wanted it the most. Never giving me what I craved. Instead, he teased. Drawing along my cotton-covered pussy, avoiding my clit in a way that had to be intentional. I arched and twisted, seeking more, but his weight on my one leg locked me into place, leaving me unable to do much more than whine and crave and soak the cotton covering me.

"Nathan, please."

He hummed, dropping his mouth between my legs and pressing a light kiss over me. "I like it when you beg me. I think I want to hear more of it."

"Nathan—" I jerked as he pressed a knuckle over my clit. One fleeting touch, then he pulled away.

"How many boys have touched you here?" he asked, running two fingers over me again. "Just the shithead, or were there more?"

I arched my back, my leg shaking. "More. Just… one more."

His dark eyes held mine, his jaw clenched. God,

he looked positively feral in that moment. Aroused and pissed at the same time. His thumb pressed hard as it ran all the way up the length of my pussy, flicking over my clit in a way that made me jump.

"How many *men* have touched you here?"

"What?" I gasped as he bit along my hip bone, such a deep, delicious, and dirty thing for him to do. It was a claiming move. An ownership bite. And I loved it. "None. No men. The only man is you."

"A boy wouldn't know how to treat this, Eve. Wouldn't know what you needed to get off. Wouldn't be able to draw it out until you were begging for it." He worked his thumb along my clit, finally giving me the pressure I'd been wanting. What I'd been needing. But before I could find a rhythm that would take me where I wanted to go, he pulled his hand away, leaning instead to rub his nose over me. "Did you let anyone taste this sweet pussy?"

Jealous Nathan was so damn hot. "No. Never."

I could have sworn he chuckled. "No, that's just for me, isn't it? I'm gonna be the only man who knows what this heaven tastes like. Who knows what it feels like when you come around my tongue."

"Only you," I whispered, tilting my hips as he pulled the fabric covering me to the side. The heat of his fingers, the roughness of his skin dragging against mine, added a whole other layer to the sensations. The feel of him so alive and hot against me with nothing in between us set my mind spinning and put my body on alert.

"Only me," he whispered before running his

fingers over my pussy again. This time, Nathan found a pattern to his movements, pushing me higher and higher as I chased that feeling. That sense of falling I knew only came from the peak of pleasure. Rubbing, sliding, breathing hard against my clit, he teased me with a single finger he pushed just barely inside. I jerked and moaned, rocking my hips, trying for more. Wanting that sensation of being filled by him.

Thankfully, Nathan gave it to me. He slipped a finger inside, pressing his thumb against my clit as I cried his name. My body tensed, my muscles readying for what was coming. Even my pussy locked down, squeezing his finger with a preorgasmic spasm that made him grunt. Made him attack my clit with his lips and tongue like a man starving for me. And maybe he was, because I'd been starving for him, too.

His tongue, his finger, the sense of it being Nathan between my legs. All of it combined to throw me right into the worst of the storm without a moment to catch my breath. I'd never come with any part of someone else inside of me, so it took me by surprise how much I liked it. How full I felt with a single finger inside. How complete.

A tornado of sensation washed over me as my orgasm hit, leaving me breathless and trembling. Nathan didn't let up for a second, pushing and teasing as he led me through to the other side. As he dragged every quiver out of me until I was a breathless, sagging mess. Completely wrung out from him.

"So beautiful when you come," Nathan said before leaning to place a kiss on my clit again. I jerked, twisting slightly, becoming even more aware of his finger inside of me. "You did good with one finger, but we're gonna need to work three in before you're ready to take my cock, aren't we, baby?"

I took a shaky breath in, trying to think. To make sense of his words. To function at all instead of simply dying inside. "I've used three."

He hummed, looking from my pussy to my face and back. "My fingers are a lot thicker than yours. We're gonna stretch this pussy out good, aren't we? Make sure you can take all of me." He leaned down and licked a long line all the way up my slit, making me shudder. His words puffed against me as he asked, "What about toys?"

I shrugged, the burn of my blush making me acutely aware of just how disheveled I had to be. My dress up under my arms, my panties shoved over to one side. "I have one, but I prefer my fingers. Always felt more real. Or what I assumed was real."

"Fuck," he groaned, looking like a man about to win the lottery. He slipped his finger from my body and tugged my panties off. I lifted a leg to help him, but he was still partially lying on my other one, which created a barrier. And an opportunity.

The white cotton of my panties rested across my knee, hanging down like a flag of surrender. Nathan's eyes stayed locked on that fabric as if it were some sort of signal. A sign. But that wasn't what I wanted him to focus on. So I let my knees fall open as he watched me, as he looked at the most secret part of me. His gaze carried a weight with it, a sensation that sent shivers shooting through my body. Every inch of me was ready for him. His touch, his lips, his gaze. I was his. Completely.

Let the storm come. I was ready for it.

Needing him to make his move, craving more from him, I bit my lip and rocked my leg until the fabric dropped lower. Until I bared myself to him. And then I smiled.

"Only you, remember?"

That did it. Nathan rolled over me with a growl, surrendering. He bit my thigh and thrust his fingers inside me like a man possessed. Two at first while his tongue tormented my clit, but as I bucked and gasped, as I moaned and cursed and grabbed hold of any part of him where my hands could find traction, he added a third. Stretching me. Filling me. Making me want to come in the worst way.

"Fuck, so hot." He pressed his thumb against my clit and worked his hand in a rocking motion. "You always get this wet?"

"No," I groaned, the sound cut off when he ran his finger along a place inside me that made my entire body jolt. He chuckled and did it again. And again. Torturing me with every thrust.

When I was almost there, clenching and crying out and desperate for release, he leaned down and placed his lips around my clit. Pressed his fingers deeper as he gave me two small licks. And then he suckled me.

I didn't stand a chance.

"*Jesus,*" he hissed against me as my body finally

arched over that precipice, as my muscles clenched down and milked his fingers. "You're going to strangle my cock, aren't you? It's gonna be heaven and hell, all rolled up in your sweet pussy."

I couldn't answer him, too caught up in the pleasure of my release. But I could reach for him, tug him by the shoulders up my body so I could wrap my legs around his hips and feel his hard cock against my still-trembling pussy.

"Please," I whispered as I leaned up to press my lips to his. "I need you. Please."

And like any person watching for an oncoming storm over the horizon, I saw the flash of what was about to happen in his eyes just before the rumble of the earth rocked us.

This was going to be a good one.

chapter seven

NATHAN

I COULDN'T BELIEVE I was here. That Eve was spread out on my bed, nearly naked and flushed. Her pretty tits heaving as she tried to catch her breath, her pussy swollen and glistening and so fucking ready to take my cock.

If I took even a minute to consider what would happen if I went through with this—*when* I went through with this…when I finally gave in to what my body'd been pushing me toward for a year—I may never. So instead I blocked it out, forced it to the back of my mind, and focused only on the gorgeous girl in front of me, begging me to fuck her.

"You still on birth control?" I asked as I stood from the bed, unbuttoning my jeans before yanking them off. I could barely get the words out, but I needed to know. There was no way I was going to fuck up her future because I was an impatient, selfish asshole. She had too much promise to be tied down with a baby right out of high school because of a moment of indiscretion. But the thought of being inside her bare, of having my come inside her all day—*fuck*. I clenched my jaw hard and willed away the orgasm that had been bubbling under the surface since the first taste of her on my tongue.

Her wide eyes met mine, then she gave a subtle nod. "How—how did you…"

"Your dad. Do you know how hard it was for me to sit there and try to console him over his baby girl going on the pill? Especially when all I wanted to do was hunt down every little bastard who'd had the pleasure of fucking you and kill them with my bare hands."

"It wasn't for them," she said. "You're the only one I've ever wanted this way. I dreamed of us like this."

"I shouldn't want you," I said as I climbed onto the bed with her, pushing her dress over her head while I nipped at every inch of skin I could get to. Licked a circle around her nipple before sucking it into my mouth. "I've tried so hard to stay away. I've tried to fuck you out of my head, but I *can't*. You're still there, with your sexy as fuck lips, your perky little tits, and that tight ass, every goddamn time. I haven't slept with anyone in nine months because it wasn't helping. None of them were you." I brushed my lips along her jaw, stroked my tongue against the shell of her ear while she shifted under me. "And now you're telling me I'm going to be the first man in this pretty little pussy?" I fisted my cock and dragged it along her slit, her eyes fluttering closed in response and a moan falling from her lips. "You're going to make me lose my fucking mind, baby."

She wrapped her arms around me, hitching her leg over my hip. Trying to get closer. Trying to get me inside. This girl was a fucking tiger on a leash. So much restrained passion.

I couldn't wait to set her loose.

"The first," she said, her heel digging into my ass. "The only."

"Oh fuck." I groaned and sank inside an inch, closing my eyes and holding her restless hips against the mattress with a firm hand. "*Eve*. You can't say shit like that. I'm going to take you like an animal if you keep it up, and I don't want to hurt you."

She clawed at my back, trying to work herself up onto my cock. Her breath caught as I sank in another inch. I was barely inside at all, and already she was like a vise around me. "I already popped my cherry with a toy. I don't care if you take me like an animal. I just want you to *take* me."

I growled low in my throat, nipping at her full bottom lip. "Let's get one thing straight, baby—a *toy* didn't take your cherry. That's all mine." And then I pushed inside more, her gasping breath the only sound she made. I watched her face as I worked myself deeper, in and out, in and out.

It was an exercise in restraint, wanting nothing more than to claim her, shove my cock in so far, she wouldn't know where she ended and I began, but knowing I needed to go slow to make it good for her. I closed my eyes and focused on her breath, the feel of her pussy squeezing me as I tried to settle in as deep I could get. She was so fucking tight, it was like fighting my way into a closed fist.

I'd been right—Eve's body was heaven and hell rolled into one.

When I'd finally worked myself all the way inside, my hips settled against the cradle of her spread thighs, she stared up at me, her eyes wide, her panting breaths brushing across my lips.

"Nathan…Nath—" She broke off on a choked moan as she clawed at my back, her fingernails no doubt leaving crescent-shaped marks on my skin. I fucking *loved* that she was marking me.

"*Jesus fucking Christ.*" I clenched my eyes closed as I struggled with my self-control. Every instinct I had was telling me to *fuck*. To pound myself into her tight little body, rut against her until I filled her with my seed. Just like a fucking animal. I swallowed down my groan. "You okay? You just tell me when, baby. I won't move until you're ready, and then I'll work this pussy so good. I'll make it feel amazing, but not until you're ready."

As much as it would cost me to stay seated inside the most perfect pussy I'd ever been in, I would. I *would*.

"Now, Nathan. Please, *now*." Her hips were restless against me, trying to work my cock even deeper than it already was.

"Thank Christ." I took her mouth in a bruising

kiss, stroking my tongue against hers as I pulled back and thrust inside, yanking her knee up and pushing it toward her chest. I slid even deeper, my groan loud and hoarse as I snapped my hips against hers at a frantic pace. I couldn't stop the overwhelming need rising up inside me to *take* her. To claim her.

Eve met every single thrust I gave, like she was seeking more. Like she needed me even deeper though she was already stuffed full of my cock. "Oh—oh God."

"Jesus, you feel so good. Better than I dreamed." I pushed inside as deep as I could and rotated my hips, grinding against her clit, making her gasp out my name. "You feel it, baby? You feel how good we fit?"

"I do. I feel it." Her legs tightened, her body beginning to tremble. "Oh God…how could I not feel it?"

"Work with me, Eve. Tilt your hips, show me how bad you want to come on my cock. You've already given me two, but you've got more in you, don't you? That hungry little pussy's been starving for me, hasn't it?"

She whimpered, trying to lift her hips against me while she pressed her head back into the pillow.

"How's it feel? Tell me, baby. How do I feel inside you?"

"Perfect. You feel perfect in me."

I dropped my head into her neck and groaned, working my hips as fast as I could, the sound of our skin slapping together echoing in the room. My need started in my toes, climbing higher, tightening my balls and making me clench every muscle in my body, trying to stave off my impending orgasm. She wasn't there yet, and there was no fucking way I was coming without giving her at least one more.

Pulling away, I sat back on my heels, choking the base of my cock with one hand while the other went straight for her clit, strumming it with quick motions.

"Nathan, what—" Her words broke off on a moan at the same time I felt her tighten up around me. She reached out, brushing her fingers against my arm, looking like I was giving her the whole fucking world. And then her eyes fluttered closed as she arched against the bed, her pussy squeezing the life out of my cock.

I didn't know where to look—at the ecstasy written all over her face, at her tits thrust toward me, or down to where I was settled deep inside her, her swollen pink lips spread wide around me, looking absolutely fucking *obscene*.

The sight of her pussy swallowing so much of my cock was all it took to send me flying. Falling over her, I braced myself on either side of her head, thrusting as deeply as I could and shouting her name as I came. Kissing away her breathy sighs, reveling in the feel of her hands stroking down my back, soothing me. Knowing even as I emptied inside her, I wouldn't be able to let her go.

Not now. Not ever.

chapter eight

EVE

THERE WERE GOOD and bad points about living with a single parent who worked all the time. The bad, well, it was pretty lonely at times. Dinners alone were the norm, and not seeing my dad for days at a time wasn't unusual. The good, though, was that he tended not to notice when I snuck in to or out of the house. A bonus, considering I'd had to find a way into the house without him seeing me after leaving Nathan's.

When I'd arrived at home so many hours after disappearing for Nathan's, my dad and Gen had been sitting in the living room together, visible through the front window of the house. She'd been talking about something, waving her hands around like she sometimes did. I hadn't been able to see his face from my angle, but he'd looked as if he'd been paying attention to her. I'd tiptoed around the corner of the house and headed for the door that led into the garage.

I owed Gen big for hanging around all day with my dad while I'd been off getting—as Nathan liked to hear me say—fucked. I needed to buy her cupcakes or tacos or a new car. Yeah, the car—that was how much I appreciated her running interference.

I'd snuck in through the side door and up the back stairs, successfully avoiding both of them. I'd almost stopped and turned around once when I'd heard my dad laugh. Truly, utterly laugh. Not the contrived chuckle he did when some business partner needed an ego stroke. A real laugh. That sound was a rarity, but my hair had been wet and my dress wrinkled—something I definitely hadn't wanted him to see.

Once in my room, I'd changed into some pajamas, crawled into bed, and texted Gen an all clear. And then I'd played through all the memories of the day. Nathan's rough hands, his gentle kisses, the way he'd sometimes lose control and grab or bite or yank. All so hot. So uniquely him. We'd showered together after, and he'd been so gentle with me. So touchy and sweet. I'd loved it. Loved him. I'd hated having to come back to my dad's house at all, and if the way Nathan had held me tight and murmured all the filthy things he wanted to do to me next time had been any indication, he felt the same. But we had to play it quiet for a while. We needed to tell my dad before he found out through any sort of gossip, but it wasn't on my list of things to do right away.

Though, apparently, telling Gen every dirty detail was—which was what she'd demanded when she'd finally texted me back, the poor girl probably stuck talking to my dad for hours about colleges and SAT scores. That was how I ended up driving to the local coffeehouse, Bundt and Grind, the next morning. She had the opening shift at the adult toy shop where she'd started working on her eighteenth birthday, so I got up bright and early, threw my hair in a messy bun, and hightailed it across the island. I'd rather have been going back to Nathan's, but he'd worked the early shift and was still on duty. I wouldn't see him for at least an hour yet. I could barely stand to wait, needing to feel his arms around me again, his weight on top of me. That slow, strong grind he did when he thrust into me.

And apparently, Gen saw that craving on my face when she walked in the door.

"You are such a slut," she said, hugging me.

I rolled my eyes, but the grin that spread across my face was unstoppable. "Shut up."

She pulled back from our embrace, looking over me with that knowing expression of hers. "You really did it."

I bit my lip. "Yeah. I really did."

"Holy shit. Holy *shit*."

"Holy shit is an understatement." I grabbed us a couple of drinks and followed Gen to the squishy chairs in the back corner, the ones that offered the most privacy and the most comfort. The soreness from the day before lingered between my legs, reminding me of what Nathan and I had done with every step. But I wasn't about to try sitting on a hard, wooden chair just yet.

"So," she said, pulling her legs underneath her. "Tell me everything."

I took a slow sip of my coffee, letting the warmth travel all the way down my throat before giving her a broad smile. "No."

"What the fuck do you mean, no?"

"No. This wasn't some hookup. It was Nathan."

"Exactly my point. Mr. Hottie Cop himself. I need dirt. Come on, spill."

"Well," I said, dragging out the word and looking to the ceiling as if I really had to think about what to say. But again, when I peered back at Gen, my grin gave me away. "He's really good with his hands. And his mouth. And…everything else."

"Everything, everything?" she asked with an eyebrow cocked.

I nodded. "*Everything,* everything."

"Well, hot damn, my little girl's all grown up." She wiped away an imaginary tear.

"Shut up."

Leaning toward me, she asked, "What are you going to tell Brock?"

I shrugged. "We're not a couple. He's been chasing after that redhead from the private school anyway. He just hangs out with me to keep the dads happy. I'll tell him we're not going to be hanging out anymore, and that'll be it."

"Sure thing. You keep telling yourself Brock

will give up when you're the one who pushes back. That's not really his personality." She took a sip of her drink, dropping her eyes to the floor. "And what about your dad?"

My stomach knotted. That was…more difficult. "I don't know yet. I can deal with him being upset with me, but Nathan's his best friend. I'm afraid of what finding out about us will do to their relationship."

"You didn't think about that before you chased after the CILF?" She rolled her eyes when I looked at her questioningly. "Cop I'd like to fuck…"

I shook my head, biting back a laugh. "I don't know where you come up with this stuff." My smile fell, all sense of fun draining away as my mind swirled with the ramifications of destroying Nathan and my dad's relationship. "I did think about it—I thought about it a lot over the past few months especially, knowing what I wanted to do once I turned eighteen. But being with Nathan took priority in my mind because he's everything I've ever wanted. I had to take a chance."

Gen's shoulders slumped a bit, her lips curving down at the corners. "Yeah, I totally get that."

If I didn't know better, I'd say Gen looked as if she understood more than she was saying. But that wasn't possible—if she had even the inkling of a crush, she told me immediately. She always had, along with every detail of every sexual exploit she'd gotten into over the years. So whatever was going on with her couldn't have been like my crush on Nathan. Which reminded me…

"Hey, speaking of my dad, I'm so sorry you got stuck with him yesterday."

She cleared her throat and shifted in her seat as she took a sip from her coffee. Shrugging, she said, "It was no big deal. We had a great talk."

I snorted. "A great talk? With my *dad?*"

"Yeah. I mean—" Whatever she was going to say was interrupted by the chiming of the alarm on her phone. "Crap."

"Time to go?" I asked.

"Yup. Gotta sell the dildos and lube." She hopped to her feet, and I did the same, both of us reaching for a hug at the same time. I wanted her to stay, for the two of us to talk more, but I couldn't get in between her and her job. She needed the money a lot more than she needed to hear me sing the praises of Nathan's tongue.

"I'll call you later, okay?"

"Yeah. Sure." She tossed her bag over her shoulder and gave me a wink. "Try to stay vertical today."

"Sure thing," I said with a shrug. "Have you seen Nathan's arms? I'd bet he has no problem with vertical positions."

"Saucy. I like it." She headed for the door with a wave and a smile, leaving me alone at the back of the shop. I grabbed our cups and headed to the counter, smiling at the barista as I stacked them on the service tray.

But when I turned back around, that smile dropped.

"You want to tell me what happened to you

last night?" Brock stood in my way, looking heated. Angry, almost. A fact that rankled.

"I didn't feel well, so I went to bed."

"Please." He led me away from the counter, back to a more secluded corner. "You were fine before you went into the house. I don't buy the whole sick excuse."

Before I went into the house…chasing after Nathan. Not that he knew my reasoning. "You don't have to buy it. All you have to do is get out of my way."

"Excuse me?" His eyebrows shot up, as if he'd never been dismissed before. And really, considering who his father was, maybe he hadn't.

But his father did business with mine, which meant I needed to tread lightly.

"Look, Brock. We both know things weren't going to work. We haven't been together in months."

"That's on you," he said, his voice hard. "I've been trying to get with you."

"No, you've been trying to get me naked. Being with me and being naked with me are not the same thing."

"Oh great." He scoffed, rolling his eyes. "Here we go with the whole prude thing. You know, maybe if you'd part those legs once in a while, you'd be in a better mood."

Asshole box…checked. Treading lightly flew right out the window. "You know what, we don't need to get into this. We're done. We've been done. We are not going to be together that way. Ever. So why don't you just leave me alone?"

I pushed past him, trying my hardest not to do something stupid. Why I had to carry the burden of my dad's business with this asshole, I had no idea, but I was over it. Nathan would never talk to me the way Brock did. He'd never treat me like I was just someone to get off with. Nathan cared, and right then, he was the one I wanted to see. Not Brock.

But what I wanted and what I got were not always the same thing.

"Hold up, Evie." Brock grabbed my arm before I could get too far away from him, spinning me around and gripping my biceps to hold me in place. "We're good together. And our dads like us together."

"So what?" I broke his hold and took a step back, trying to hide the way my hands were shaking. "We are *not* together and never really have been. Besides, I want someone else."

Brock's face burned red as his eyes pinned me in place. "Are you fucking cheating on me?"

Crap. I shouldn't have brought up someone else. Nathan and I weren't ready to tell anyone about us yet. If Brock figured out who was in the kitchen with me and that we both disappeared at the same time, we were in trouble.

I shook my head, trying to figure out an escape path. "No. I just—"

"Who is it?" He herded me back against the wall again, his voice quiet but hard. Dangerous. "Some kid from across the river? Is it that football player you were talking to last year?"

Shit. This was bad. Brock had me tucked into

a corner, out of sight of the barista station and at an angle where anyone looking probably thought we were enjoying a little private time. There was no way past him—my only way out was right through him.

"No," I said, putting my hand on his chest to ward him off. "You're being an asshole and need to cool down. I'm leaving now."

"Fuck no, you're not." Brock shoved me against the wall. Everything about his closeness felt wrong—he didn't smell like Nathan, didn't touch me like Nathan would. He was not who I wanted, but I had no doubt he didn't care. I pushed against his chest, but he kept coming. Bringing his head down to try to steal a kiss. I turned, refusing him, but he caught the corner of my mouth. Just the feel of his lips so close to mine made me sick.

Using every self-defense skill Nathan had taught me when I was younger, I pushed and blocked, finally managing to get both hands between us. When I had leverage, I shoved, pushing him away. "Stop it, Brock."

Brock didn't move much, but he did step back enough to give me an opening to run. I wiped my mouth with my thumb, looking toward my escape just in time to see the door open. To see Nathan walking in, wearing his uniform and looking absolutely delicious. Until he took off his sunglasses.

His eyes were wild, filled with a rage I'd never seen before. And they were directed right at me.

chapter nine

EVE

LETTING EVE LEAVE last night had been one of the hardest things I'd ever done. I'd desperately wanted to keep her locked up in my house and never let her go. Handcuffed to my bed would only be an added bonus. It was as if all the feelings I'd repressed for a year were making up for lost time, overflowing and pouring out of me. Making me crazy when it came to her.

Now that I knew what she smelled like in the crook of her neck, knew the taste of her against my tongue, knew the sounds she made when she came, I was so far gone for that girl there was no turning back.

I was hers, completely.

I glanced at my watch as I left Maxine's Market. There'd been a string of vandalism recently to some of the shops downtown, and I'd wanted to check in with the owner and make sure things were okay. I had less than an hour until my shift was over, then I had major plans for the next twelve hours that included nothing but a naked Eve.

Knowing I was going to need all the strength I could get for the things I planned to do to her later, I made a detour to Bundt and Grind to grab a quick cup of coffee. As soon as I walked into the place, I scanned the room, a habit ingrained in me for as long as I could remember. It was as busy as I would expect it to be this close to noon. Sam was working today, and I waved as I headed that way when something in the back of the shop caught my eye.

Eve stood frozen, Brock behind her, his arm outstretched toward her, his jaw clenched. She swiped at her mouth as she darted her eyes around, and then she looked my way. As soon as I took in the sheer panic written all over her face, I saw red. That fucker had done something to put that look on her face. I pulled my sunglasses off as I stalked toward them, clenching and unclenching my fists as I went.

"Nathan, it's not—" Eve started, but my focus right now was on getting this asshole as far away from my girl as possible.

"You," I said, grabbing him by the collar of his shirt.

"What the hell, man?"

"Shut the fuck up." Wrapping my fist around the collar to make it tight against his throat, I tugged him toward the front door, Eve trailing behind, repeating my name. I could barely hear her over the blood pounding in my ears, the urge to knock out every one of this little bastard's teeth thrumming in my veins. I wanted nothing more than to put the look of panic Eve wore on his face instead.

I yanked open the door of the coffee shop and shoved him outside, making him stumble on the sidewalk.

He spun around to face me, smoothing out his shirt as he did so. "I can't believe you just did that! Do you even know who my father is?"

"I don't give a fuck who your father is," I said, pushing him away from Eve. Just to get more space between them. Every nerve ending in my body was begging me to fight. To *protect*. But the three of us were under a microscope right now, drawing the eyes of several onlookers downtown, not to mention the people who'd been seated in the coffee shop when I'd dragged his ass out. Because of that, I couldn't slam his face into the brick building. Couldn't break every bone in his body. Couldn't smear the sidewalk with his blood. "If you ever even *look* at her again, I will come after you without this uniform on. Do you understand what I'm saying? I'll hunt you down until it's just you and me, and then we'll see how many different ways I can make you bleed. Am I making myself clear, you spoiled little fucker?"

He paled, nodding quickly before turning on his heel and scurrying in the opposite direction from where I left Eve.

Eve.

I whipped around, frantically searching for her. She stood off to the side, her eyes wide. I couldn't read what that look meant, but I didn't have it in me right then to try. She wiped the back of her hand against her mouth again, like she was trying to erase the taste of something foul, and I narrowed my eyes as I stalked over to her.

"Did he hurt you?"

She dropped her hand to her side. "No, he—he tried to kiss me. But I turned my head. He just grazed my lips."

That fucker'd had his lips on *my* girl. *Forced* his lips on her. If we weren't the focus of a dozen onlookers, I would've wiped his taste from her lips right then and there. I needed to get her out of here, as fast as possible if I had any hope at all of not taking her up against the front windows of Bundt and Grind.

"Get in, Eve." I jerked my chin toward my car.

"But my car—"

"I don't care about your car. Get in. *Now.*"

She startled at the harshness in my tone, shrinking back, and that killed me. Fucking *killed* me. That flinch made me feel like the biggest asshole in the world, despite the fact that all I wanted to do was protect her. The red haze that had overtaken me at seeing Brock advancing on her receded enough that I could contain the rage boiling inside me as I walked toward her.

Balling my hands into fists so I didn't reach for her, didn't lift her against me and carry her off to where I knew she'd be safe, I lowered my voice so only she could hear. "I walked in on him reaching toward you and *you* looking terrified as hell. And now I just found out that he *kissed* you? He touched what's *mine*? I'm hanging on by a thread here, baby. I need you to get in the fucking car. *Please.*"

Parting her lips, she stared at me for a moment before nodding. I opened the door for her, slamming it shut once she was inside. Circling around the hood, I ignored the commotion the encounter had caused and attempted to get myself under control, but it was like trying to contain an erupting volcano. All I could see was the look on her face, eyes darting around the coffee shop in a panic as she'd tried to flee. *Fear.* She'd been scared, and I hadn't been there to help her.

"Nathan," she whispered, brushing her fingers against my forearm.

I gripped the steering wheel until my knuckles turned white. "I can't right now, Eve."

She must've heard the desperation in my voice because she didn't say any more, letting her fingers drop from my arm as she stared out the window. I wanted them back on me, wanted her touching me everywhere. I wanted to pull over and take her against the hood of my car, not caring who could see. *Wanting* people to see, just so they'd know she was mine.

By the time we pulled into my driveway, my need was so strong I could barely hold myself together. This urgency to *claim* was something I'd never felt with anyone but her. Despite the view in front of me—Eve walking up *my* path into *my* house—I still couldn't stop the incident from replaying in my head. Him looming over her. Her terrified face. Me being too far from her to do anything.

But here, now, I couldn't get my hands on her fast enough.

Before the back door was shut behind me, I had her in my arms, her tits pressed against my chest and her ass cupped in my hands.

"Nathan," she managed to get out before I sealed my mouth over hers. She moaned into the kiss, sliding her tongue against mine as she wrapped her arms and legs around me.

I pushed her against the door, pinning her in place with my hips as I devoured her mouth for long moments until she was gasping for air. "Don't want you to taste anyone but me. Don't want you to remember anyone's hands on you but mine." I reached under the hem of her skirt, sliding my fingers along the seam of her pussy through the cotton of her panties. "Jesus, you're wet already. Tell me this is for me, baby. Tell me."

"It's for you. It's always for you," she said, her head tipped back against the door as I licked up the length of her neck.

I needed to get at more skin, needed to feel her against me, but I didn't want to take my hands off her. Couldn't stand the thought of putting her down even to get her naked. Bracing her against the door with my hips, I gripped the front of her shirt and tugged it apart, snapping buttons off until her chest was bared.

"Nathan!"

"I'll buy you another," I said as I pulled the cup of her bra down and sucked a nipple into my mouth, then did the same on the other side. Her little hips worked against me, grinding her pussy down on my cloth-covered cock. Like she couldn't wait. Like she needed me inside her as desperately as I needed to be.

"You need my cock again?" I blew against the nipple I'd just licked a circle around, causing it to harden even further.

She whimpered and scraped her nails down my chest, her fingers tracing around my badge, biting her lip as she stared at me.

"Tell me you need it, baby. Tell me you need me." I was a selfish fuck for asking this of her. For not staying away in the first place, but I couldn't. Not anymore.

"I do. I need you, Nathan."

I clicked the button on the front of my belt buckle and let my uniform pants fall to the floor with the weight of my gear. Shoving my boxer briefs down far enough to free my cock with one hand, I hoisted her up with the other, then pulled her panties to the side. I sank inside in one deep thrust.

"*Christ.*" I glanced down to where she was wrapped around my cock. "I didn't think it could get better than yesterday, but I was wrong. This pussy's welcoming me home, isn't it?"

She gasped, digging her nails into the back of my neck as she stared at me, flushed and fucking perfect. I gripped her hips, keeping a barrier between her and the door, protecting her from the punishing rhythm of my thrusts as she moaned into my mouth. The kiss was sloppy, her movements uncoordinated as she tried to match my pumping hips before finally giving in and letting me work her how I wanted. My hips slapped against her inner thighs, and some sick part of me hoped I'd leave marks. Wanted her to have a little reminder of me only she could see.

But I wanted a reminder *everyone* could see, too.

Bending my head to her neck, I sucked a patch of skin into my mouth, sinking my teeth in before soothing it with my tongue. "If he ever comes near you again, you tell me. Do you understand? You fucking tell me." I worked myself into her faster. Harder. Deeper. Until I felt her clenching around me, her moans nearly nonstop. "You're *mine*. I tried—I tried so hard to stay away. I *should* stay away, but I'm not strong enough. Not strong enough to walk away from you now. I can't. I *can't*."

"So don't. Stay with me." She brushed her lips across my ear, her breathing erratic. "Stay with me, Nathan." And then she was coming around me, her pussy squeezing me so fucking hard, I couldn't do anything but follow her.

"Always," I groaned, thrusting deep and spilling inside her. "Always."

It didn't matter if being with her might cost me the most important relationship I'd ever had. Would probably cost me that. I loved Brandon like a brother. He'd been there for me through every shovelful of shit tossed on me during my life. He'd been the only constant, the only *family* I'd had.

But none of that mattered. Not in the face of Eve.

Nothing would matter if it meant I had to be without her. If it meant I couldn't have her by my side. She was mine, and I'd fight for her if I had to.

chapter ten

"WE NEED TO get out of bed."

Nathan kissed his way up my neck, running his hands over my breasts in a rough sort of possessiveness that had me arching into his touch. "No, we don't."

His thigh pressed against my pussy, and I nearly screamed. I was so sensitive from yesterday and this morning. If he pushed me any harder, I'd probably give in to him. But not yet. "Nathan."

"Eve." He pressed his lips to mine again, his weight pinning me down. His entire body practically enveloping mine. I loved him like this—all affectionate and demanding. Refusing to let me out of his sight. I understood it, too, after the situation with Brock this morning.

But…

"I'm starving." That came out as more of a whine

than I'd intended, but I couldn't help it. My stomach was growling. "We need to eat lunch."

Nathan sighed in an exaggerated way, as if the thought of food was too much of a bother. "Fine. My baby needs food. But after that, it's back to bed and no clothes for the rest of the day."

I wouldn't have had it any other way.

Nathan pulled on a pair of threadbare sweat pants that hung low on his hips and, with one final kiss, headed for the kitchen. The sight of his tight ass rolling, the muscles of his back flexing, and the tattoo that covered his left arm—*my* tattoo—almost made me regret letting him leave the bed.

I tossed on one of Nathan's T-shirts—almost giggling at how it hung to my knees—before heading for the front of the house. As happy as I was with Nathan, though, a sense of anxiety haunted me. I couldn't stay here forever, no matter how much I wanted to. Not until we talked to my dad. Nathan pulling Brock out of the coffee shop would be major grist for the gossip mill within hours. Even my work-obsessed dad would probably hear it and know something was up. Especially if he spotted my car parked downtown where we'd left it. Not that I expected him to—he'd probably be at work until late in the evening like always.

Still, we needed to sit down with him, to explain things, to reassure him that we were happy together. But even the thought of starting that conversation made me sick to my stomach. Not to mention the fact that Nathan and I needed to have some serious conversations about our plans. How could we be so committed and so up in the air at the same time?

"Eggs okay?" Nathan called from the kitchen.

"Yeah. Sounds good. I like mine—"

"Scrambled with red pepper flakes. I know."

And he'd have his over easy with so much pepper they were almost black. The benefits of having known your new lover all your life—little things like food preferences didn't need to be discussed.

As Nathan opened cabinets and banged around in the kitchen, I headed for the back hall. Discarded clothes left a trail all the way to the bedroom, and buttons littered the floor. A sure sign of a good time had by all, if I did say so myself. Still, it was a bit of a mess. Might as well make myself useful.

I was on my hands and knees collecting buttons when the back door swung open.

"Nate. I can't find… Evie?"

Oh God, that voice. It was the last thing I wanted to hear considering I probably looked as if I'd been doing exactly what I had been doing. Having lots of sex…with Nathan. His best friend.

My dad froze just inside the door, his polished loafers stepping on one of the buttons from the shirt Nathan had ripped off me. There was no way this was going to go well.

I sat back, took a deep breath, and peered up into the eyes of my father. He took one look at me, and his face went red.

Shit. "Dad, it's not what—"

But I was too late to smooth this over. He

grabbed my arm and pulled me to my feet, scattering all the buttons I'd collected across the floor again. The move was so sudden, so swift, I couldn't help myself. I yelped. A crash came from the kitchen, and then the sound of Nathan's running footsteps grew closer.

"Eve!" Nathan raced around the corner, grabbing me and pulling me behind him probably before he even saw who was with me. In what felt like a split second, his hands ran over my body as he shoved me deeper into the house, keeping himself between my dad and me. When he seemed sure I was okay and there was enough distance between me and the supposed threat, he whipped back around. "Who the fuck—"

"You bastard." My dad stepped forward, shoving Nathan hard. "I heard you pulled Eve and Brock out of Bundt and Grind. Do you have any idea how panicked I was when I saw her car there but couldn't find her? I come here looking for help, and you've got her barely dressed and on your floor like some sort of…" He huffed a breath, glaring down at my naked legs under the hem of what was obviously Nathan's shirt. And then he yelled, "She's my fucking daughter!"

My dad charged, and I stumbled back, the force of the two crashing together almost knocking me over. Regaining my footing, I spun into the living room, still unable to look away from the fight. But I couldn't really even call it a fight. My dad swung, hitting Nathan square in the mouth one time. To my surprise, Nathan didn't duck, didn't even try to defend himself. Just took the punch my dad dished out.

Nathan's head snapped toward me, then rocked forward once more. Swiping his thumb across his lip and smearing blood along the way, he flicked his eyes up to mine before turning back toward my dad, still holding me behind him. "I deserved that. But that's the only shot I'm giving you."

"You don't need to give me shit, asshole. You think you can touch my baby and get away with it? I'll have your ass thrown in jail."

"Dad, stop." I slid between them, arms out, hoping like hell they could both just settle down.

Nathan tried to yank me behind him again. "Eve, no."

I smacked at his hands, refusing to hide from my own father. "It's fine, Nathan. Dad, he never did anything wrong."

"What do you know, Evie? You're just a dumb kid when it comes to men," Dad roared.

Once again, Nathan shoved me out of the way, putting himself between my dad and me. "I don't give a fuck if she's your daughter. You're not going to talk to her like that, not in my house."

But my dad had known Nathan most of his life, had probably fought with him a time or two. He didn't back down. Instead, he inched forward, standing toe-to-toe and glaring at his best friend. "I'll have you strung up in the center of town."

"No." I grabbed Nathan by the arm, my fingers

spread across the face of the woman in his tattoo. My hold solid over his sign of love for me.

"Let go of him, Evie," my dad said, almost growling the words.

But I couldn't let go. I wouldn't. I held tighter, clutching Nathan like a lifeline. "No, Dad. You're so wrong about this. I'm an adult, and this relationship was my choosing. Being with Nathan forever is what I want."

Nathan's muscle twitched beneath my fingers as his head whipped around. His brown eyes met mine, so much emotion in them. So much heat. "It is?"

My dad huffed, ignoring Nathan's question. "You can't know that—you're only eighteen."

But I didn't care. Nathan was looking at me as if I was the only thing he wanted, the only thing he needed in the entire world. As if he couldn't believe I would choose him.

"I know I love him," I said, refusing to break Nathan's gaze. Needing him to understand my declaration was as much for him as for my dad. "I know there's no one else I'd rather be with. And I know he's the one person who could ever make me happy."

My dad groaned and started to pace. "This is bullshit, Nate. You're too fucking old for her."

Nathan just kept staring down at me, looking so damn disbelieving. The fire there, the need…that look was everything to me.

"I'm not good enough for her," Nathan said, his voice too deep. Too honest. Speaking to me as much as my dad. "I'll never be good enough, but I'd rather die than hurt her."

"And when she leaves?" my dad asked. "When she heads off for college this fall?"

"It doesn't matter. Wherever Eve is, I'll be." He gave me a tiny smile, a private one just for me before meeting my dad's eyes. "I can't be without her, Brandon. I know that's not what you want to hear, and it's not what I want to say. But I wasted so much time fighting it, I'm not going to waste another minute not being with her. I love her."

"Really?" The word was out before I could think about it, before I could try to filter it.

Nathan wrapped one arm around my waist, pulling me closer into his body. "Was I doing a poor job of showing you that? Yeah, really."

I grinned and rose onto the balls of my feet, needing to be closer. "*Really*, really?"

He ducked his head closer, his lips brushing my ear as he whispered, "Now that I've had a taste, I can't give you up."

"I don't want you to." I dropped back down, flushing as I caught my dad glaring from only a few feet away. "And you don't need to go anywhere. You can stay right here."

My dad raised an eyebrow as Nathan frowned.

"I'm going to go to Temperance Falls College," I said, making sure my voice was firm. "I don't want to leave the island, so I'm staying here."

"What?" Nathan asked, looking almost as if he didn't want to believe me. "But Eve, you should—"

My dad cut him off as he said, "You should go to a better school away from here. Experience life before someone"—he waved at Nathan, glaring again—"traps you into a life less than you deserve."

"I deserve a life filled with love," I said, letting my voice grow louder. Letting my frustration at years of always being second place to his dreams and his career boil over. "I want to be someone's first priority, not their burden. I want to know what it feels like to be taken care of and loved. I want to live the life I've always dreamed of, with family and friends and people who come home from work and actually want to spend time with me. That life includes Nathan—it requires him. If I ever decide I want more and need to chase after it—"

Nathan grabbed my hand. "I'll chase right after you."

"I know," I whispered. Because I did know. Of that, I had no doubts.

"I never meant to leave you alone so much," my dad said, suddenly sounding almost sad.

"But you did. I get it—you had your own dreams to fulfill. You wanted the occupational success and the power that came with your name on the letterhead where you worked. Those are good goals to have. They're just not for me. Being with Nathan is my dream. The life he can give me is the only thing I want."

My dad sighed and ran a hand through his hair, looking completely lost for a moment. "Fine. If this is what you want." He pinched his eyes closed for a second before shooting daggers at Nathan once more. "I don't like it. I don't. She's an adult, so I won't stand in her way. But I don't forgive you for doing this. And I swear to God, if I find out you touched her one second before she turned eighteen—"

"I didn't," Nathan said. "And I hope you know enough about me to know I'm a man of my word. I said I wouldn't hurt her, and I won't. I'll spend the rest of my life working to make her happy."

My dad just shook his head. "Man, if Evie weren't here, I'd beat the fuck out of you."

"Dad—"

"Do it," Nathan said, moving in front of me. "Take your best shot. I gave you one already before you knew the situation. I'll give you one more now that you do."

My dad clenched his fist, looking ready to attack, but then he glanced at me. I hung over Nathan's arm, peeking out from behind his muscles with my hands still on that tattoo. Hoping like hell the two didn't dissolve into a fistfight.

Dad held my gaze for a long, tense moment before unclenching his fist. "I won't upset my Evie that way. But I will tell you this—you step one fucking toe out of line with her, and all bets are off. She's going to school. She will graduate. And you will do everything in your motherfucking power to make her happy, or you'll be dealing with me."

Nathan gave a short nod. "Understood."

I rushed forward, wrapping my arms around my dad's neck and pulling him into a hug. "I love you, Dad."

"I know." He pushed me back, refusing to look at me. "I love you too, Evie, but I can't deal with this right now. I need a little time to accept it."

With nothing more than an arm squeeze for me and another glare shot at Nathan, he turned and stormed out the door.

"That went…" I trailed off, not sure how to assess the situation.

"Better than I expected," Nathan finished for me. He grabbed me by the arm and spun me around, lifting me right off the ground with a hand cupping my ass. "So, you love me, huh?"

"I do." When I said the words, his eyes lit up. "And you love me."

He leaned in close, kissing me with enough passion to set my soul on fire. His hands kneading my ass, he stroked my tongue with his. Teasing me.

"Nathan," I moaned when he moved to my neck.

"There you go, grinding your pussy on me again. You need my cock already? Did me telling you how much I love you get you hot to fuck?"

Such a filthy mouth. But I was learning. "No, you telling me you love me didn't get me hot. Your thick cock rubbing up against me did." I leaned in and nibbled on his earlobe before whispering, "You've got me so wet, Nathan. What are you going to do about it?"

We were in motion before I got the final word out. Nathan carried me right to the bedroom, no more questions, no more words. Once in the room, he dropped me onto the mattress and moved to crawl over me, but I didn't want that. I rolled him over, straddling his hips. He looked up at me with what I could only describe as wonder. Which was probably exactly the way I looked at him.

"My turn to be in control." I rocked once, rubbing myself over where he was so hard for me.

"What about your breakfast?" he asked, the way his hands gripped my thighs and moved me against him telling me exactly what he thought—or rather didn't think—about breakfast.

But my hunger didn't matter anymore. At least, not my hunger for food. My hunger for the man I was smiling down at was a whole different matter.

"We'll have breakfast for dinner."

epilogue

NATHAN

I WASN'T SURE how I'd lasted twelve months staying away from Eve, because the five days between her telling me she loved me and her permanently moving in to my house had been the longest five days of my life. I understood where she was coming from, wanting to allow Brandon a little time to get used to the idea of her and me together. Her relationship with her dad had always been distant, and this didn't help. She didn't want it to be damaged beyond repair.

I understood it, but that didn't mean I had to like it.

All I knew was she was mine, and that meant I wanted her in my arms, in my bed, in my house. To hell with everything else, even if that *everything else* was my best friend.

But now she was here, her hair piled on her

head, a tank top molded to her tits, her legs looking a mile long in the pitiful excuse for shorts she was wearing. Looking hot as hell. Looking fucking *perfect* in our house, despite trying—again—to haul the boxes into our bedroom that her dad was piling in the hallway.

"Eve," I snapped when she reached for another. "Stop trying to lift the fucking boxes."

She huffed and rolled her eyes, crossing her arms against her chest. "I'm not weak. I can handle lifting some boxes."

"I never said you couldn't." I stacked the box I was carrying on top of the one she'd tried to lift and hauled them both down the hallway to our bedroom.

"Show off!" she called after me, bringing a smile to my face.

After dropping off the boxes, I headed into the living room, coming face-to-face with Brandon as he set down one at the edge of the hallway. He hadn't said anything, but he hadn't had to—he might as well have drawn a line on the hardwood floor showing how far he was willing to step into the house now that Eve was living there. Apparently, the bedroom was a no-go zone. Couldn't blame him—not after what I'd done to her in there last night.

Thoughts of her on the bed filled my head— her arms stretched overhead, wrists cuffed to the headboard, her legs spread, eyes hooded. But I shut those memories down before I could recall in great detail the feel of her pussy clenching around me, how she'd screamed my name when she came…

The last thing I needed right now was to get hard in front of her father.

"That's the last one," he said, stuffing his hands in his pockets and looking everywhere but at me.

Thankfully, Eve came around the corner from the kitchen and tipped her head in the direction of the box her dad had set down. "Is that it?"

"Yeah, pumpkin," Brandon said, brushing past me to get to Eve. "I'm not doing anything with your room at home, so if things don't work out…"

Eve glanced at me, smiling. "Thanks, Dad. But I'm sure I won't need it anymore."

I snapped my mouth shut and clenched my teeth so hard they hurt. What I really wanted to say was, "Yeah, fucker. She's sure." But I wasn't going to add fuel to an already raging fire. Not when the person it would harm the most was the one I never wanted to hurt.

Brandon huffed. "Yeah, okay. Just…don't be a stranger."

"Never." She rose up on her feet to kiss his cheek. "I'll come for dinner this week."

"After you finish registering at Temperance Falls College."

"Dad," she said, rolling her eyes.

"No. That's the condition. I'll accept this whole thing if you go to school. Period."

"Fine. I'll come by for dinner after I register so you can see my schedule."

Eve's phone rang, interrupting the moment. She pulled it from her pocket and frowned at the screen. "It's Gen," she said to us as she walked toward the kitchen. "Hey, why aren't you here?"

I watched her walk away, partly because I loved her ass in those shorts and partly because I couldn't stand to take my eyes off her even for a second. When she was around the corner, I turned back to find Brandon looking to where Eve disappeared before meeting my eyes. For the first time, he didn't look furious. He didn't even look hurt. He looked… resigned.

I dropped my arms from the defensive stance I was in and scrubbed a hand over my head, blowing out a deep breath. Eve was the best thing that had ever happened to me, and I wouldn't change that for anything. But the friendship Brandon and I shared had been going on for longer than she'd been alive. I owed it to both of us to try to repair whatever I could.

"I'm not sure what she said or did to make you change your mind about all this," I said, waving a hand around to indicate the two of us, "but it means a lot to her, so it means a lot to me. Thanks."

"Yeah, well…I'm still not okay with all this. But I know you make her happy. Finding the person who does that…it's sort of a gift. No matter how messed up it makes things, you can't turn your back on it."

The way he said those words set off my instincts, something in the tone of his voice indicating he wasn't just blowing smoke up my ass but was speaking from experience. Before everything that had gone down with Eve, I would've asked him about it. Hell, before, he would've told me about it. But we weren't there now. I didn't know if we ever would be again.

He lifted his eyes to glance over my shoulder, his brow creasing. I turned to see Eve coming back into the room, staring at the phone in her hand, a frown marring her face.

"Baby?" I asked. "What's wrong?"

"Gen's mom was in a car accident. Her leg's messed up, and she has to have surgery."

"Shit," Brandon hissed. "What can we do?"

"Gen asked me to pick up toiletries and some comfortable clothes since she's going to be staying at the hospital for a while."

"She's alone?" Brandon asked.

"Yeah. I mean, it's just the two of them and—"

"No." He ran a hand through his hair, looking distracted as he started patting his pockets like he was searching for his keys. "I'll go sit with Gen. You get her what she wants from her house. And food. She needs food. Maybe those chocolate candy ball things she likes so much."

"Dad," Eve said, following him. "What's up?"

"Nothing." He said it a little too quickly, but Eve didn't seem to notice as he cleared his throat and met my eyes. He stared at me for a moment, then glanced at her before looking back to me. "I don't want Gen left alone at a time like this."

Without saying another word, he strode out the front door, shutting it behind him. I didn't know if it was the cop in me, or the fact that we'd been best friends for two decades, but I picked up the signals he was giving off loud and clear.

Brandon was sweet on his daughter's best friend.

Seemed we had a lot more in common now than we ever had before.

Eve looked toward where her dad just left, her forehead creased. "That was weird."

"Was it?" I asked, brushing the hair away from her face. I bent and ran my nose up the length of her neck, breathing her in. *Apples.* "What's weird is that I haven't fucked you yet today."

She put one hand flat against my chest, but she didn't push me away. "Nathan, I told Gen I'd be there soon."

"Mhmm, but your dad'll be there with her for a bit. Besides, soon doesn't mean now. Soon could mean an hour." I gripped her hips and walked her backward down the hall to the bedroom. Bending down, I nipped at her bottom lip, then hauled her up against me, lifting her off her feet because I couldn't stand not touching as much of her as possible. "I can do a lot in an hour, baby."

the
DILF
LONDON
HALE
keep reading for a sneak peek

chapter one

BRANDON

THERE WAS SOMETHING disturbing about walking into a hospital when your reasons for being there were completely in the wrong. Still, I did it. Climbed out of my car after rushing across town, all because of a phone call. I'd seen this sort of nonsense on dramatic television shows—the whole one moment changes your life bullshit. But I guess it wasn't bullshit, not really. Should have been. Would have been, but then I'd spent an evening with someone I shouldn't have been alone with, and as cliché as it sounded, my world changed. My focus changed. In all the wrong ways.

So when the phone rang and the news that Lara McKay—mother of my daughter's best friend—was in a horrible accident, that new focus sent me scurrying to find out what I could do to help. But again, for the wrong reasons.

Yes, Lara was hurt. Yes, she needed someone to check on her since she had no family here except her daughter. Yes, my being her daughter's best friend's father gave me access to more of her life than a casual acquaintance, so I felt comfortable coming when I found out about the accident. That was all fine. What wasn't fine was the reason I chose to come to the hospital—because it wasn't Lara.

It was her daughter.

Genesis.

One of the sexiest human beings I'd ever had the unfortunate luck to come across. Fiery, wild, bold— Gen wasn't a woman you could ignore. Especially not when she turned those huge blue eyes on you. It was impossible. Until you remembered she was eighteen years old. Then…not so impossible. Hard for sure, just as she made me every time she looked my way, but not impossible.

Yet there I was, storming into the hospital because I knew she'd be alone. I knew she'd need someone. And I wanted that someone to be me.

"Lara McKay," I said as soon as I approached the information desk. The man behind it, who wore an obnoxiously decorated sticker with the name Paul in the middle of it, frowned and typed, frowned and typed. Slowly. If he'd been an employee of mine, I'd have fired him already. And that was before he started humming to himself.

"Car accident," I said, doing my best not to grit my teeth. "Came in through the emergency room."

He nodded and pressed a few more buttons at

the pace of a sloth. "Got it. Looks like she's in the surgical ward. Are you family?"

"Yes, I am." The lie came easily—too easily—but the fact that my own cousin was a surgeon here had taught me a few things. Like that only family was allowed in the surgical waiting room, and that the volunteers behind the desk would never ask for proof of relationship.

Paul did not disappoint. "Perfect. Okay, here's a guest badge. Please wear it throughout the hospital. Surgery is up on—"

"Four," I said, cutting him off as I snatched the plastic badge from his fingers. "Yeah, I got it. Thanks."

I rushed to the elevators and jabbed the up button more times than necessary. The damn thing seemed to take forever to arrive and even longer for the doors to slide closed behind me. What was it with this place and obstacles?

As I stared at the lights telling me what floor we were on, my impatience burned hot under my skin, my need to get upstairs harsh and painful. I would've liked to have said it was for Lara. She was a nice lady, pretty and sexy. Between her looks, her charm, and the fact that we were the youngest parents on the PTA—fully a decade younger than the rest—it would have made sense for us to date. Hell, we'd even flirted a bit when the girls first met and we started seeing each other at playdates and birthday parties. Two single people in their early twenties trying to navigate the waters of being a parent and an adult tended to gravitate together. But no, she wasn't for me. No one had been, really.

I'd kept any romantic connections private—very private. Temperance Falls was a small island with big eyes and even bigger ears. The last thing I needed was to start dating someone and risk my reputation. I had a little girl to raise, one I protected with everything I had. Lara had been barely more than a blip on my attraction screen.

Her daughter was a whole different story, and I was going to end up in hell for the thoughts I'd had about her. Those thoughts—fantasies, if I was being honest—had started recently. Really recently. Just since the night barely over a week ago, when she'd sat on my couch talking with me as if we were old friends. Leg up and tucked beneath her, far too much skin on display, red hair tumbling over her shoulders—she'd been a dream come true. A siren calling to the basest parts of me. And smart. The girl was charming, personable, witty…and sex on legs. I'd barely been able to resist her; the only thing keeping me from pinning her under me was the knowledge that my own daughter, Gen's best friend, had been sleeping upstairs at the time. That and the fact that she was far too young for me. Probably.

Think of the devil, and he shall appear…

"Brandon." Genesis caught me as I stepped off the elevator, those killer eyes meeting mine. They were so bloodshot, so pained, so worried. I couldn't help myself. I grabbed the girl and pulled her into a hug, shielding her as much as I could with my body.

"Are you okay?" I asked, nearly shaking with my need to press myself against her. To feel more of those curves. To hold her tight and never let her go so I didn't have to think about what would have happened if she'd been in the same car as her mom when it went over the bridge. Fuck, she wasn't mine in any way, but that would have killed me.

Gen clutched my shoulders, her delicate fingers pressing deep, and nodded against my chest. "I'm fine. My mom's bad, though. There's swelling around her brain, plus her leg's pretty mangled. I don't… I'm not sure what we're going to do."

The fear in her voice gutted me. "It's okay. It'll be okay."

A silent moment, the feel of her body melting into mine, and then she cried. Hard. Fuck, that wasn't like Gen. The girl was loud, brash, and audacious. Sexy in a way that stopped men in their tracks. I'd done a good job of ignoring those facts as she grew into them, but then last week, after Evie's graduation party… I couldn't ignore them anymore. And I hated myself for thinking about that while she sobbed in my arms. Asshole of the Year award, well deserved.

A polite cough had me turning, though I didn't let go of Gen. I kept her wrapped up and safe. Close to me.

"Hey, Brandon." My cousin stood before me looking tired and slightly curious. Of course, he did—I had a sexy-as-fuck eighteen-year-old in my arms. Shit.

"Josh. Good to see you." I reached out a hand, moving Gen into my side so our embrace looked a little more appropriate. Which was fine so long as no one noticed the massive fucking hard-on I was now sporting. "How's Lara doing?"

"She's hanging in. Her lower left leg is broken in three places, and her MCL is completely torn. We have the best orthopedic surgery team on their way in to take care of that, but it's not our priority." He glanced at Gen, who was still tucked against me with her hand on my chest. "Your mom took a pretty solid hit to the head, and that's the issue we need to address immediately. There's a lot of swelling, and that can cause brain damage, but this isn't a touch-and-go situation. We'll relieve the pressure by opening up a flap in her skull and keep her unconscious for a few days to give her brain time to heal."

Gen felt rigid in my arms, so I jumped in with the first question I needed answered. "So, you're operating today. When will they operate on her leg?"

"The team should be here tomorrow."

The single parent in me couldn't help but ask, "And what's her recovery timeline?"

Josh held my gaze, his concern obvious. "Minimum two weeks in the hospital, then another two to six in rehab. It depends on the amount of damage—if any—to her brain."

Four weeks minimum. Gen could end up alone, without someone to look over her, for a month. In the back of my mind, I knew she didn't need another person around, but that didn't appease the instinctual part of me that didn't want her unprotected.

"Okay." Gen pulled away from me before I could decide what to do about the four-week thing, squaring her shoulders, a little of that fire back in her eyes. "When can I see her?"

Josh frowned, shooting a look my way before refocusing on the woman before him. "You can see her now, but only for a few minutes. I want her in an operating room within the hour."

"Fine. Let's go." Gen snatched her bag off a chair, then reached as if to grab my hand. Looking somewhat lost. Somewhat vulnerable. Looking as if she needed me. "Come with me?"

Fuck, the dirty places my brain went when she said that, when she looked at me like that. How could I possibly tell her no?

"Of course."

We followed Josh to a room off the main hallway. The place was dim, almost dark, but not enough that we couldn't see the woman huddled under the sheet. Couldn't see the bruises and cuts, the pillow-like device holding her leg in place. Gen stiffened when she walked in, completely froze for a moment as she took in the sight of her mother so damaged. I squeezed her hand and hoped my presence offered at least a modicum of comfort.

"Five minutes," Josh whispered as he caught my eye. "I'll talk to you later?"

I nodded, knowing that talk would be about why I was touching a young girl who wasn't my daughter. Shit, a woman. I needed to remember that. Gen was eighteen.

Just like my daughter.

Who was fucking my best friend.

When had my life become a soap opera?

"Mom," Gen whispered, leaning over the bed. I stayed back, kept out of the way. Gave the two ladies their space. Lara's eyes fluttered a few times before finally opening, focusing in on her daughter immediately.

"Gen." Her voice was rough, pained. Too quiet. "You okay?"

Gen huffed a laugh. "You were the one in a car accident, but you're asking if I'm okay?"

"It's the mom in me. I can't help myself."

"I'm fine. How are you?"

"I feel like I got hit by a semitruck and fell off a bridge. Oh wait, I did."

"Mom, be serious."

"Fine. I feel like ass. Everything hurts, even focusing my eyes."

"The doctor's going to fix you."

"I know." She licked her lips, glancing my way. "Brandon, can you take her?"

My eyes darted to Gen before returning to the patient. "Lara?"

"I don't want her home alone for days on end. Can you take her? Let her come stay with you and Evie?"

Temptation had a way of making you do things you shouldn't. Wrong things. I should have told Lara that Evie no longer lived with me. That maybe Gen staying with me—the man who had jacked off to thoughts of her every day for the past week—wouldn't be a good idea. The right thing would have been not to lust after a teenager.

I did not do the right thing.

"Of course. Gen can stay with me as long as she'd like."

Gen stiffened, her shoulders going tight as she glanced back at me, then addressed her mother. "Mom, no. I can stay at home by myself. I'm almost nineteen. I don't need a handler."

"I know you don't, but I'd feel better if I knew you were taken care of." She flicked her eyes in my direction, and my guilt multiplied. "Otherwise, I'm just going to be in here, worrying about you."

The fight in Gen went out as soon as her mom spoke the words. "Fine. But promise the only thing you'll think about while you're in here is getting better."

"I promise. I know Brandon will take good care of you."

Yeah, I would. Hopefully without letting her know how much her curvy little body turned me on. How hard it was for me not to reach out and touch every inch of her pale skin. How fucking hard she made me every single day.

There was no denying it. I was going to hell. One I created for myself.

Buy it now to keep reading!
www.londonhale.com/thedilf

about the author

London Hale is the combined pen name of writing besties Ellis Leigh and Brighton Walsh. Between them, they've published more than thirty books in the contemporary romance, paranormal romance, and romantic suspense genres. Ellis is a *USA Today* bestselling author who loves coffee, thinks green Skittles are the best, and prefers to stay in every weekend. Brighton is multi-published with Berkley, St. Martin's Press, and Carina Press. She hates coffee, thinks green Skittles are the work of the devil, and has never heard of a party she didn't want to attend. Don't ask how they became such good friends or work so well together—they still haven't figured it out themselves.

www.londonhale.com